AN AVALON ROMANCE

SPANISH SERENADE
Alba Marie Pastorek

S Budding opera singer Dallas Jones and her aunt, Eula, are touring Spain when they are involved in a car crash. When dashing, mysterious Rick Santana appears with offers of help, Dallas is instantly suspicious. With nowhere else to turn, she allows him to escort her to his luxury hotel, steeling herself against his Latin charms.

As if one alluring Spaniard weren't enough, Dallas meets Maestro Miguel Rivera, the brilliant director of the Opera Company of Seville. To her surprise and delight, Miguel offers her a plum role in *Don Giovanni*.

While rehearsing with the company, Dallas discovers that a thief has been stealing jewels from the opera's prima donna, Estela, who also has her eyes on Rick. Could this be the same thief who's robbed Rick's hotel? How will Dallas solve the mystery while withstanding Rick's relentless pursuit and Estela's haughty jealousy? Her Spanish serenade turns out to be the most complicated song she's ever sung!

SPANISH
SERENADE

●

Alba Marie Pastorek

AVALON BOOKS
NEW YORK

Poem on page 18 from "Sonatina"
(1893) by Rubén Darío

PRINTED IN THE UNITED STATES OF AMERICA
ON ACID-FREE PAPER
BY HADDON CRAFTSMEN, BLOOMSBURG, PENNSYLVANIA

In loving memory of
John J. "Jack" Pastorek,
who always encouraged his children to read, write, travel and sing.
1923–2000

Chapter One

"Señor!" Dallas Jones cried, close to hysteria. "Wh-what are you doing? Where are you taking my aunt?!"

Dallas's blurred gaze followed the raven-haired, broad-shouldered giant as he strode purposefully toward the sleek silver Mercedes that was parked in the dust beyond the crumpled pickup truck. She watched in a daze as the dark stranger barked instructions to the group of arguing, swarthy-faced men who surveyed the chaotic scene. The stranger looked about thirty-five, but his commanding tone instantly garnered the older men's attention. One dashed forward to open the rear door of the Mercedes. A moaning Eula Weber, her arms and legs dangling like a broken puppet's, was carefully eased onto the backseat of the luxury car.

The truck had been laden with cages of chickens, and dozens of recently released birds were clucking and fluttering around the accident site. Chattering on-lookers milled about, some waving in disgust at the pileup of crushed vehicles, others commiserating over the damage done to their own automobiles. The poor, elderly truck driver made a rather comical addition to the scene as he chased after his flock of runaway poultry, Spanish expletives spewing from his wrinkled mouth.

Gnawing her lower lip, Dallas ignored them all, save the man who, moments before, had inserted his head into the compact rental Toyota, assessed Eula's condition in an instant, and promptly carried her off.

The afternoon summer sun glared mercilessly on so much confusion, and Dallas felt a sheen of perspiration dampen her bruised forehead. Shielding her eyes with one hand, she blinked to regain her focus before moving on trembling legs toward the Mercedes. The dark stranger had just finished arranging Eula on the seat and was closing the rear door.

Thus far he had appeared grim and silent—except for the curt order he'd issued to the men—and he had barely spared a glance in Dallas's direction. She decided he was either deaf or he didn't understand her frantic English interrogation. Nevertheless, she tried again in a voice quavering with shock and anxiety.

"Please, *señor* . . . what are you doing with my aunt?"

He pivoted from the car and paused to regard Dallas evenly. His substantial height, over six feet, forced her to crane her aching neck in order to meet his narrowed, steel-gray gaze.

"What am I doing?" he said dryly. "Isn't that obvious, *señorita*?" His rich baritone voice startled Dallas with its lack of accent. "The woman may be seriously injured. She should see a doctor as soon as possible." His black brows sloped critically in his aristocratic bronze-skinned face. "Would you prefer to wait for an ambulance, which could take an hour or more to arrive?" he drawled, impatience in his tone.

"No, no, of course not," Dallas replied, raising a shaky hand to brush the silky pale strands framing her forehead. In doing so, she exposed the ugly bruise discoloring the skin above her right eye.

The tall stranger stepped forward. "You've been hurt, too," he murmured with concern. "Here, let me take a look." Then his strong, lean fingers were encircling the nape of Dallas's neck before his words had even penetrated her disoriented brain. Gently, he urged her face heavenward by pushing his thumb against her jaw. Her shoulder-length blond hair tumbled away from her ashen cheeks, and she found herself staring mutely at the muscled column of his throat while he examined her. Affected by his proximity as much as by his exploring touch, which seemed to linger longer than necessary, Dallas's heart thudded with alarm against her ribs. To augment her distress, she was finding it increasingly difficult to breathe normally. His face was so close to hers, the tang of an expensive aftershave filled her lungs.

She winced, her velvety lashes fluttering, when his fingers probed the purplish bump crowning her eyebrow. "Sorry," he said, releasing her. "Come on . . . we need to get both of you to a hospital . . . *pronto*."

Dizzily, Dallas glanced around for a last look at the mangled navy Toyota. It was crunched between a white Fiat and a larger car she couldn't identify. So many vehicles had been involved in the pileup, it would probably take hours to pry them apart.

The stranger gripped Dallas's arm and marched her to the passenger side of the Mercedes. She watched him grasp the door handle, her attention drawn to the sleeve of the cream dress shirt where an initialed gold cuff link glinted as it caught the sun.

Then he was urging her into the cool leather and chrome interior of the elegant car, and her concentration shifted abruptly back to her injured relative. She swung round in the seat and peered at Eula Weber's recumbent form. Relief brightened Dallas's worried blue eyes when the petite woman raised her salt–and–pepper head and attempted a pained smile.

"Auntie, please don't try to move, okay?" Dallas instructed anxiously. Her glance skimmed the older woman's red polyester-clad figure for signs of damage.

"Not to worry, hon," Eula replied, her usually robust voice decidedly weak. "I declare, I feel like half the bones in my body are cracked."

Then the driver's door was being whisked open by

their mysterious rescuer who slid lithely behind the steering wheel. Dallas had a split second to assess his profile—the aquiline nose, well-molded lips and strong jawline—before he was turning to fix his intent gaze on her. It briefly and dispassionately swept over her floral-print cotton sundress, down her bare legs and sandaled feet and back up again to rest on her wan face.

"What about your handbag, *señorita?*" A sudden frown slashed his tanned forehead, bare except for an errant fork of thick, straight, ebony-dark hair.

"Huh?" Dallas was so absorbed in her dazed study of his striking Latin features that she was staring in bewilderment.

"It occurs to me that you were probably traveling with a handbag ... a purse of some sort?" he said calmly.

Eula groaned while Dallas looked stricken. There were dozens of people swarming around the wreck. At the rate their luck had been going, their valuables would be history for sure. Dallas made a grab for the door handle, gasping when the stranger's hand restrained her. His warm fingers were firm yet gentle against the bare skin of her arm.

"You stay put," he instructed. "I'll be back in a minute." Dallas watched him exit the Mercedes. He was shaking his head as he approached the remnants of their ruined transportation.

"Do you suppose he regrets playing the Good Samaritan, Dall?" Eula Weber's hazel eyes twinkled in spite of her discomfort. "The poor man must think we're a couple of silly, helpless females."

"*Poor* man?" Dallas echoed, shifting her squinting gaze from the scene outside. "From the looks of him—and this car—I'd say he isn't even vaguely familiar with the word, Aunt. But never mind him . . . how are *you* feeling?"

"I'm afraid this leg is shot," Eula replied, gingerly stroking her left thigh. "It's probably broken."

Their self-appointed benefactor reappeared and deposited two worn leather shoulder bags onto the front seat.

"Thank you so much, mister . . . ?" Dallas paused, realizing she didn't know his name.

"Santana—Rick Santana—at your service it seems, ladies." He took his place behind the wheel, turned the key, and the powerful car purred to life.

"I'm Eula Weber, and that's my niece, Dallas Jones. Needless to say, we are forever in your debt, young man," Eula spoke from the back seat. "To think we might still be stranded, unable to drive that demolished rental car."

"If I hadn't happened by, someone else would have assisted you, I'm sure, Señora Weber," Rick Santana rejoined. "You'll find that our people are very compassionate and always willing to aid tourists in distress."

He was a native, of course. Dallas hadn't doubted that for a second, considering his virile Iberian looks. Yet his English was flawless and curiously devoid of accent. And although his surname certainly sounded Spanish, his first name did not.

"Well, we're very grateful to you, *señor*," Dallas said, trying to ignore the nagging throb in her head.

"I'm glad I could help," he replied, and after a pause inquired, "Where are you ladies from?"

"Texas . . . Austin, Texas." Dallas smothered a small troubled sigh. Home seemed a million miles away at the moment. An accident like this back in the States would have been upsetting; in a foreign country, the ramifications were magnified tenfold. "What about you?" She opted for conversation to distract herself from this depressing reverie. "Where do you live?"

Rick Santana raised one large hand to indicate the shimmering city sprawled ahead against the rose, gold and copper horizon. "There . . . the capital of *Andalucía—Sevilla*—or Seville, as it's known to the English-speaking world."

The stretch of highway Eula and Dallas had maneuvered from Córdoba was soon abandoned for wide boulevards congested with noisy traffic. As the city unfolded before them, Dallas briefly regretted leaving the sun-creased countryside of Spain. She had fallen in love with the magnificent scenes of rugged mountain ranges, burnished fields of wheat and sunflowers, and fertile slopes studded with olive trees and vineyards. However, in no time she found herself equally impressed with the beauty of Seville. Lovely gardens and tree-lined *plazas* abounded, interspersed with ornate churches and old and new buildings displaying a variety of architectural styles. Still, her concern for Eula remained paramount in her weary mind.

Presently, Rick Santana swept the Mercedes into a crowded parking lot adjacent to a four-story brick building occupying an entire block of one busy avenue. He set the brake, saying, "Stay with your aunt, *señorita*. I'll get some help." With that, he slipped out of the car and was gone.

Minutes later he returned, accompanied by two white-shirted young orderlies. "*Cuidado, hombres—* be careful," he instructed in a deep, crisp voice. Eager to comply, the men carefully lifted Eula, placed her on a wheeled gurney, and rolled her toward the emergency room entrance. Dallas was right behind them, Rick Santana at her side.

"You'll need to be examined as well," he remarked when they reached a pair of swinging aluminum doors.

"I'll be okay," Dallas said. "My head's a little sore, that's all."

"The doctor can take a look at you when he finishes with your aunt."

Dallas shot Rick an annoyed glance as they continued down a sterile-smelling hallway, but she decided not to comment. Eula would think it ungracious to argue with the man after he'd been helpful enough to drive them to the hospital.

They followed the orderlies down another corridor before reaching a small examination room where Eula was gently transferred to a hospital bed. Dallas was alarmed to note the pallor of the older woman's face, and she moved quickly forward to grasp her aunt's hand.

"How are you doing, Auntie?" she asked anxiously.

"I'll be a heck of a sight better as soon as you lose that worried look, Dall," Eula retorted. She sought Rick Santana's amused gray eyes over her niece's narrow shoulders. "Would you kindly get her out of here and tell the doctor I'm waiting?"

Dallas felt their new benefactor take her arm. His possessive touch, although seemingly impersonal, affected her in a curiously disturbing way. Her pulse skittered and she was at a loss for words.

They were met just beyond the door by a balding distinguished-looking man clad in a white coat, a blue shirt and a striped silk tie.

"Ah, Ricardo . . . *señorita*. Here you are." Kind brown eyes smiled through wire-rimmed glasses as the doctor accepted the younger man's hand.

"It's good to see you again, Roberto. Please meet Miss Dallas Jones from Texas," Rick said, adding, "This is Dr. Hidalgo, Chief of Staff here at Santa Cecilia."

"Mucho gusto, señorita." The friendly doctor squeezed Dallas's outstretched hand. "If you are from Texas, you must surely speak a little Spanish, eh?"

"I wish I could claim more than my limited vocabulary," Dallas admitted ruefully, "but I'm afraid I studied French and Italian in school."

"How interesting," Roberto Hidalgo rejoined politely. "Well, I am always pleased when I have the opportunity to practice my English. Now if you will both excuse me, I will look in on the other American lady who, I hear, is in distress."

"Thank you so much, doctor," Dallas said, managing a troubled smile. She watched as he passed into the room and introduced himself.

Again, she felt Rick Santana's affecting touch at her elbow as he led her down the corridor and past several rooms before locating a vacant waiting area.

After they were seated, Dallas twisted sideways to ask him something about their rental car, and her head spun dizzily and she moaned. Blinking, she attempted to bring Rick's frowning face into focus.

"What is it? What's wrong?" he demanded. Shifting to the edge of his chair, he turned and grasped her upper arms to support her wilting figure. "I'm getting the doctor—*now*."

"No—no, please . . . I—I'll be okay . . . in a second," she protested feebly. Her pounding head was drooping, but the wave of nausea was ebbing. She inhaled slowly and straightened, willing her swimming vision to clear.

"You're as white as these walls," Rick murmured. His concerned gaze roamed her delicate features, lingering on the long sable-brown lashes that splayed shadows across her high cheekbones, and her full, yet innocent mouth. His lean hands maintained their hold on her. Even in her woozy state, Dallas was alert to the branding warmth on her bare skin as she rested her head on the wall. Her eyes remained closed, but she could feel his assessing gaze on her pale oval face. Suddenly, the giddiness she felt was more the result of his nearness than any injury sustained in the accident.

Her heart commenced an erratic beat, and she experienced an abrupt and urgent need to be free of his touch. "I—I'm feeling much better now," she said breathlessly. Her eyes fluttered open and she shrank a little away from him.

Rick got the message immediately. His black brows quirked in a fleeting frown as he dropped his hands and settled back into his chair. "So tell me, how long have you and your aunt been touring Spain?" His tone was coolly polite.

"Oh, about a week and a half." Dallas told him how she and Eula had flown into Madrid and rented the car, deciding to travel south down to Córdoba and Seville, then east over to Málaga and Granada, then north along the coast to Barcelona. They had planned a leisurely month in Spain, followed by a week on the French Riviera, and intended to finish up the summer in Italy.

Before Rick could comment on the itinerary, Roberto Hidalgo appeared.

"How is she, doctor?" Dallas asked, rising on wobbly knees.

"She will be fine—in time, *señorita*. I've given her a mild sedative and something for pain, and she's resting peacefully now. Unfortunately, there is the problem of what on the surface appears to be a broken ankle. We will know for certain as soon as the x-rays are complete."

Dallas's eyes widened with concern, but she listened wordlessly to the rest of his report.

"I will need to keep her here for several days at the very least. Depending upon the bone damage, she may require crutches, or perhaps even a wheelchair."

Dallas sighed heavily. "Poor dear. She was really looking forward to this trip. I suppose we'll just have to return to the States as soon as she's able to travel."

"That must be your decision, *señorita*, but for now I do not want your aunt doing anything more than resting. She looks to be in good health, but an accident such as this is a shock to anyone's system. And Señora Weber is not—how do you Americans say?—a spring chicken?" The doctor's warm brown eyes remained serious.

Dallas found herself dimpling despite their dilemma. "I wouldn't let my aunt hear you say that, doctor."

Rick Santana had been silently witnessing their exchange. He wound a comforting arm around Dallas's shoulders. "You don't need to make any major decisions tonight," he said. "Why not wait and see how you both feel in the next few days, hmm?"

"You're right," Dallas murmured, thinking out loud. "I'll stay here with Aunt Eula, and tomorrow we can discuss our next move."

"I'm sorry, *señorita*, but you cannot remain at the hospital overnight," Dr. Hidalgo informed her apologetically. "Unlike many medical facilities in your country, we do not have accommodations for visitors at Santa Cecilia."

"But how can I possibly leave my aunt here alone?" Dallas queried in dismay. "She doesn't speak a word of Spanish. . . ." Dallas glanced hopefully up at Rick for support, tiny worry lines etched at the corners of her wide blue eyes.

But to her chagrin, he declined this time to come to her aid. "Don't insult the good doctor," Rick reprimanded her lightly. "Your aunt will be expertly cared for throughout the night, isn't that so, Roberto?"

Dallas's gaze flitted from one man to the other, catching the older man's affirmative nod, his kind, patient expression. As for Rick Santana, he casually ignored the resentment she shot at him.

"But I don't know where to stay," she protested, again thinking aloud. "We had planned on a small bed and breakfast on the outskirts of the city, but now I'll need to be near the hospital—"

"That's not a problem," Rick interposed smoothly. "I'm taking you to the Palacio Moro."

"Palacio Moro?" Dallas repeated, her nervousness growing.

"One of Seville's many hotels," he said matter-of-factly. "It's little more than a mile from here."

"And what am I going to do about the Toyota?" she exclaimed, abruptly remembering they had simply abandoned the rental car. "I'll need to contact the auto agency to inform them of the accident." Her pretty face clouded over. "They'll probably want a police report, and—"

"I'll take care of all that," Rick interrupted briskly.

"Let Roberto examine you so I can get you to the hotel."

In light of her heightened apprehensive state, his authoritative tone triggered a shrill warning note in Dallas's overwrought brain. Exactly who was this large, rakishly attractive man so determined to whisk her off to a place called the *Palacio Moro*—'Moorish Palace'? With his expensive clothes and confident air, Rick Santana resembled a wealthy playboy, perhaps even an unprincipled Casanova in search of a young, gullible victim.

In a desperate attempt to disguise her mounting uneasiness, Dallas forced a tone of concern, asking, "Haven't we imposed on you enough for one day, *señor*? You've already been extremely helpful."

Rick's firm lips twitched in a knowing smile that sent Dallas's pulse racing. "It's no imposition, honestly, *señorita*," he drawled quietly. "I'll just wait for you here, hmm?"

Dr. Hidalgo gave Dallas a clean bill of health and some pain tablets for her headache, promising he would take excellent care of her aunt. Before she joined Rick Santana in the waiting area, she looked in on Eula and found her sleeping peacefully in her small private room.

"I'll be back first thing in the morning," Dallas assured the doctor, shaking hands with him. "Thank you again."

"*De nada, señorita. Hasta mañana* . . . and please do not worry. Señora Weber will be fine, and I have the number of the hotel if we need to contact you for any reason."

Night had fallen on Seville, and the historic city glittered in nocturnal splendor as Rick propelled the Mercedes down a broad avenue. He was curiously silent, and Dallas used the time to speculate about who he was and where he was taking her. She cracked the window at her right, inhaling deeply to dispel some of her anxiety. The warm summer air was thick with the mingled perfume of orange blossom and jasmine.

He braked the car at the gleaming entrance of the most elegant hotel Dallas had ever seen. Its stunning façade was designed like that of an Arabian palace, complete with intricately carved arches supported by slender white marble columns. It reminded Dallas of guidebook pictures she'd seen of Seville's Alcázar and Granada's world-renowned Alhambra.

A smiling, black-jacketed male figure appeared at Dallas's door and whisked it open with a flourish. *"Bienvenido, señorita,"* he welcomed her with a bright smile. Her apprehension growing by the second, Dallas slowly stepped out, but remained standing by the car.

"Hola, Señor Santana," the doorman cheerfully greeted Rick who was circling to Dallas's side. She remained glued to the cement at her feet, even when she felt Rick lightly grasp her arm.

Chewing her bottom lip, she glanced up at him, found something undefinable in his narrowed gaze, and promptly gave in to the panic that had threatened to overwhelm her since they'd left the hospital parking lot.

"I'm sorry . . . I—I can't stay here!" she exclaimed, jerking her arm from his hold. Wide-eyed, she backed away from him as if suddenly discovering his resemblance to Jack the Ripper.

"Really? And why not?" he questioned in a low tone, a slight frown creasing his handsome face.

"It—it's just too expensive, that's all," Dallas stammered. "I couldn't possibly afford to stay here."

"Listen, don't worry about that," Rick said casually. Moving closer, he took her arm again and drew her toward the entrance, fronted by a beautiful Oriental rug. "Just consider your room and board on the house, okay?"

"I don't think so!" Dallas snatched her arm from his grasp and glared up at him, mutiny in her enormous eyes.

Rick towered over her, his expression marked by surprise. "What precisely is the problem, *señorita*?" he asked quietly.

"I'll find my own place," she retorted, declining to answer him. How could she admit her suspicions concerning his reasons for taking her to this fabulous, obviously expensive hotel? Through the wide glass doors beyond the marble façade, she could see colorful ceramic tile and luxurious carpeting. Sparkling crystal and brass chandeliers hung over a vast lobby alive with activity.

Clutching her shoulder bag to her midriff like a shield, Dallas glanced anxiously around, praying that a taxi would suddenly materialize. All she saw was a long white limousine pulling up behind the Mercedes. The black-coated young man, grinning now, was holding the door in anticipation of Dallas's entrance. Two other uniformed male employees were camped behind a small reception desk, whispering and watching with amusement. Still, she refused to budge.

"There's a very nice restaurant just inside," Rick remarked coaxingly, evidently deciding to pacify her. "I'm sure you could use something to eat. Why don't we discuss your accommodations over a cup of coffee and a sandwich?"

This suggestion sounded innocuous enough not to send Dallas into a flurry. "All right," she grudgingly agreed. What else could she do? The prospect of a taxi ride to a low budget hotel in an unfamiliar city was most unappealing, and she was famished. She and Eula had snacked on cheese and crackers in the car, but that had been hours ago.

Again, Dallas felt Rick Santana grasp her arm to lead her into the Palacio Moro. Taking a deep breath, she shook aside the sudden disquieting premonition that there would be more to remember about the famous Spanish city of Seville than the inconvenience of an automobile accident . . . much more.

Chapter Two

"**P**obrecita princesa de los ojos azules," Rick Santana quoted softly, gazing at Dallas from across their corner table in the hotel's brightly-lit coffee shop. It was a large, informal restaurant with flowering hanging baskets throughout, smiling waiters and waitresses bustling efficiently around crowded tables, and patrons noisily conversing in a multitude of languages.

"What does that mean?" Dallas inquired suspiciously. She busied her nervous hands by flipping through a menu that featured everything from omelettes, called *tortillas*, to American hamburgers.

"It means 'poor little blue-eyed princess,' " Rick translated. He continued his intent regard, his firm lips slightly curved in amusement.

Pink color instantly stained Dallas's cheeks. "I'm

18

not a princess—little, poor or otherwise, *señor*," she informed him in a tight voice.

He chuckled. "You know, I believe you're the first woman I've ever offended by quoting a line of poetry." He paused while a young waitress placed mugs of steaming coffee in front of them. "I apologize," Rick went on after the girl had departed, "but you reminded me of the princess in that poem. She longed to be a butterfly or a swallow so she could fly away."

"I don't get it," Dallas said irritatedly. Beyond exhaustion, her head ached miserably, and she resented him for making light of her disturbing circumstances. And she didn't trust his motives for bringing her to the Palacio Moro either.

"Oh, come on, Dallas. Admit that you would like nothing better than to run away right this minute . . . from me?" His smiling eyes teased her mercilessly.

Dallas remained silent, her heart in her throat. She wasn't about to acknowledge how skillfully he had read her thoughts.

"What are you so afraid of? That I plan to exact some sort of non-monetary payment from you in exchange for a room in this hotel?" Rick's amused gaze raked suggestively over her, from the top of her blond head down her blushing face and slender neck.

"That's ridiculous. I'm not afraid of anything," she snapped, her color flaming to crimson. *That's exactly what had gone through her confused brain!*

"What a little liar you are, *chica*." Rick gave a short laugh. "You're feeling trapped and afraid because your aunt's familiar presence has suddenly been replaced by that of a dark foreigner."

"Maybe I am a little . . . uncomfortable," Dallas retorted, her delicate chin jutting out defensively. "I don't know you from Adam. You appear from out of nowhere after the crash—"

"And rush you to the hospital," he interrupted her soundly, "make arrangements for your car, and offer you safe accommodations. For this you choose to attach ulterior motives to my behavior. Are you always so mistrustful—so suspicious?"

Only with tall, dark, handsome men, thirty–ish and sophisticated, Dallas was thinking, her heart thumping with alarm. Strangely, this one's bold appraisal unnerved her more than an audience of five hundred at the university theater where she'd performed countless times.

"I—I don't mean to seem ungrateful," she blurted hastily. "As Aunt Eula said, we do owe you a great deal. But I don't wish to be any more beholden to you than I already am. And if I allowed you to pay for my room—"

Their waitress arrived in response to Rick's beckoning gesture. "*Sí*, Señor Santana?" The dark-eyed girl nodded obediently as he spouted a rapid stream of Spanish, not a word of which sounded familiar to Dallas. Then, to Dallas's surprise, the girl hurried from the coffee shop.

Seconds later another equally attractive young waitress glided over to take their order, attentive to every word uttered by Señor Santana. He was obviously one of the restaurant's regular customers, because the staff seemed to know him by name, including a stunning, smiling brunette who suddenly appeared at his side, demanding, "Ricardo, where have you been all day?" She bent to plant a brief kiss on his tanned forehead, turned and grinned knowingly at the pretty blond sharing his table. "Never mind that question. I think I can answer it myself."

"Pull up a chair and meet Miss Dallas Jones, from the great state of Texas," Rick drawled.

The young woman obeyed at once. "It's a pleasure, Dallas. I'm Anita Santana, this *hombre*'s baby sister." She flashed a warm, friendly smile, her black-lashed green eyes meeting Dallas's curious stare.

Thank heavens she seems nice and normal, Dallas thought with relief, murmuring a hello and returning Anita's smile. The Spanish girl, who looked to be in her late twenties, bore little resemblance to her brother, except perhaps for the aristocratic bone structure of her striking golden-skinned face, and the fact that she spoke the same impeccable, unaccented English. Her chin-length hair, a deep brown shade with reddish highlights, was a stylish mass of curls crowning her proud head. She wore a tailored beige linen suit over a tangerine silk blouse, and coral lip gloss glistened on full, sensuous lips.

"So what's up, *hermano*?" Anita Santana's attention returned to her brother, who briefly related the events of the afternoon, pausing at intervals when his sister would animatedly issue an "oo" or "ah." When he concluded, Anita turned to Dallas.

"You poor thing! What a perfectly dreadful day," she exclaimed. "Of course, you must stay here at the Palacio with us. You can use the spare room across the hall from mine."

"You're living here . . . at the hotel?" Dallas asked, really puzzled now.

"Why, yes. I'm the assistant manager of the Palacio Moro."

"I see," Dallas murmured, actually not seeing anything at all. Surely being an employee in a hotel didn't automatically entitle one to a free room.

"Anita, I think Dallas might be confused by the fact that you reside in the hotel." Rick's amused gaze remained fixed on Dallas's bewildered face.

"That's simple," his sister explained. "The Palacio Moro belongs to Rick—he owns it. We both live here. Didn't he tell you?"

After Dallas regained control of her mouth, which had dropped open in amazement at that bit of information, she replied: "No, I guess he just didn't get around to mentioning that." Her low voice was controlled, but she shot Rick a venomous look his sister immediately understood.

"Oh, I get it," Anita said. "Let me guess. He had you thinking he was one of our local lotharios, right?" She glowered at her brother, who was leaning back in his chair, his arms crossed, the picture of innocence.

"Something like that," Dallas admitted, her accusing gaze locking with Rick's laughing eyes.

"Well, that's my dear big brother's perverse sense of humor for you. Pay no attention to him."

"Hey, now wait a minute." Rick straightened to protest. "I can't help it if she has an overactive imagination." His even, white teeth glinted as he grinned.

"You know darn good and well you deliberately let me think the worst," Dallas snapped, her delicate brow knitted in anger. A sharp pain rocketed through her head and she groaned, both hands flying to massage her temples.

Rick rose, issuing sharp instructions. "Anita, see that her room is ready. She needs to go to bed. And tell Isabel to send the food upstairs."

"Sure thing, Rick." His sister flashed Dallas a brief, anxious glance, then hurried to comply.

Dallas sat hunched over, head in her hands, her stomach tied in miserable knots. "I—I'll be fine . . . in a minute," she mumbled, when she became aware of Rick looming over her. Rising tentatively, she groped for her leather bag slung over the back of the chair. When Rick's steadying hand clamped around her upper arm, she tried to shrug it off, still unbelievably irked with him for his little joke.

"Come on. Let me help you, *chica*," he said in exasperation, maintaining his firm grip while they sidestepped between people and tables. When Dallas's purse slipped off her shoulder, landing with a thud on the tile floor, a plump-faced, white-haired woman reached down to retrieve it.

"Here you are, honey," the elderly tourist said, her concerned gaze running over Dallas's blood-drained face.

When Dallas twisted her head to thank the woman,

a wave of dizziness crashed over her, and she swayed. Moaning, she felt herself and her purse lifted into Rick's powerful arms. His warm breath stirred the pale hair on her forehead as he muttered something indistinguishable in Spanish. *He's probably cursing my ancestors*, Dallas reflected hazily.

Her head was throbbing in an agonizing rhythm— a combination of the blow received in the accident, and the fact that she hadn't eaten for hours. With a slight troubled frown, Rick strode briskly across the vast lobby of the hotel, encountering startled and curious glances from employees and guests alike, all of which he imperiously ignored.

"Please . . . please, put me down," Dallas protested wearily. Her aching head rested in the crook of his broad shoulder and the strong column of his throat. Her bare slender arms were limply draped around his neck.

"If I put you down," Rick murmured near her ear, "you'd just fall, and I'd have to pick you up again."

He was undoubtedly right, darn it all. Even in her weakened state, Dallas couldn't help but appreciate his clean masculine scent mingled with that expensive after-shave or cologne. She felt fragile and boneless, overcome by the intoxicating warmth of his gentle strength. Oddly, her recent anger had evaporated into thin air.

Rick took the hotel's wide, regally carpeted staircase in lieu of a line of crowded elevators, carrying her with remarkable ease. "You weigh little more than a child, *pequeña*," he commented against her hair. "How old are you, anyway?"

"Old enough to be embarrassed about being hauled through a public place like a sack of groceries," Dallas complained in a little voice against the collar of his shirt.

Rick's wide chest rumbled with amusement. "Come on now, tell me how old you are? I'm thinking you can't be more than nineteen or twenty."

"Twenty-five," Dallas admitted, lulled by the steady drum of his heartbeat against her side. At another time, she might have haughtily informed him that she had a masters degree from the University of Texas, was working on her doctorate, and had probably performed in more musical productions than he had ever attended in his thirty-plus years.

"Still a little girl," he teased softly, his arms tightening possessively around her. Against her will, Dallas felt her skin growing warm with secret pleasure. There was something incredibly seductive about being manhandled so tenderly by this large, confident male.

No expense had been spared in making every room and suite in the Palacio Moro as impressive as the splendid hotel's sumptuous lobby and three restaurants. Dallas's room, plushly carpeted in rich teal, contained a queen-sized mahogany bed decorated with a royal blue quilted spread. A pair of heavily lined ivory drapes framed a sliding glass door that opened to the second-floor balcony. Opposite the bed was a lovely Persian rug beneath two velvet-upholstered armchairs and a carved oval coffee table, providing a convenient sitting area to enable guests to enjoy their meals in style without ever having to leave the room, if so desired.

Rick carefully lowered Dallas's feet to the carpet next to the bed. Maintaining his protective hold on her, one hand was flattened against her back, the other cupped the nape of her neck. Dizzy with fatigue, she blinked up at him, her heart racing at the piercing intensity of his narrowed eyes. She caught her breath, suddenly aware of the unexpected intimacy of being positioned against his hard, muscled length. He was probably supporting her so she wouldn't crumple, but his hold on her had all the qualities of an embrace. And the fact that he didn't immediately release her seemed to suggest that he was deliberately prolonging the moment . . . perhaps to gauge her reaction.

Her fluttering gaze landed on his firmly molded lips. To her shock and dismay, she found herself wondering what it would be like to experience the feel of his mouth on hers. Terrified that her pounding heart would give her away, Dallas shrank in his arms, her hands instinctively lighting on his chest in a posture of defense.

"What is it?" he demanded in a husky voice, searching her face with his critical gaze. "Why are you looking like that?"

"Like wh-what?"

"Like you're afraid of me again?"

"I've already told you—I'm not afraid of you," she insisted, the faint tremor in her voice belying her words.

"I think you are." A challenging light glowed in his charcoal eyes. "And if you weren't about to drop at my feet, I might be tempted to test my theory . . . right here and now." His silky tone, and the fact that his arms tightened ever so slightly around her, sent her nervous system into overload.

"Please . . . I really *am* exhausted," Dallas murmured breathlessly. Her quivering fingers pushed weakly against the solid wall of his chest.

"Sorry." Rick's arms retracted so abruptly that her legs buckled beneath her. She collapsed onto the edge of the bed. Her head reeling, she grabbed for the adjacent bedside table to keep herself upright in a desperate attempt to preserve her dignity. When she squinted up at him, she saw an inscrutable mask descend over his good-looking, aristocratic features.

"Your dinner should be here in a minute," he announced quietly. "Why don't you eat something, take the medicine Roberto gave you, and try to get some sleep."

Dallas took a deep breath. She steeled her voice to be steady so as not to betray how emotionally distraught she was feeling. "That sounds like a good plan," she responded.

"Good night then." Rick turned away from her and headed for the door.

"Thank you again . . . for everything," she said.

He glanced back over his shoulder. "No problem, *señorita* . . . sleep well." With that, he closed the door behind him.

Less than five minutes later her suitcase and Eula's

were delivered to the room by a cheerful bellhop. Delighted to have her belongings back, Dallas perked up at once. She guessed that Rick had telephoned from the hospital and instructed a member of his staff to deal with the damaged rental car and the luggage.

The food arrived next—a cheese and potato omelette with a fresh salad and a Coke. Famished, Dallas ate hastily before swallowing one of the pills Dr. Hidalgo had given her. She was already feeling better, so she extracted Eula's guidebook on Spain from one of the cases, flipped to the chapter on Seville, and found herself not at all surprised to learn that the five-star Palacio Moro, with its several hundred rooms, outstanding service and international cuisine, was considered the city's top hotel. After kicking off her dusty sandals, she wearily headed for the large tub in the immaculate white-tiled bathroom. Throughout her relaxing bath and until her weary head settled into a plump pillow, Rick Santana remained foremost in her thoughts . . . so much so, in fact, that his darkly handsome face lingered to haunt her in troubled dreams.

Dallas stirred reluctantly at the insistent jangle of the telephone on the bedside table. Yawning, she groped for the receiver and murmured a muffled hello.

"*Buenos días*, Dallas. It's me, Anita. How are you feeling this morning?" The voice on the other end of the line chirped cheerfully, evidence that the effervescent assistant manager had been awake for some time.

"Uh, better . . . much better, thanks."

"Did you sleep well?"

"Like a rock," Dallas replied, slowly sitting up amidst the tangle of sheets and blanket.

"I'm glad to hear that," Anita said. "You needed a good night's rest after your ordeal yesterday. Listen, I thought you might be ready for some breakfast since it's nearly ten."

"Ten!" Dallas's leaden eyelids flew wide. "Poor Aunt Eula probably thinks I've abandoned her! I have to get to the hospital—"

"There's no need to rush," Anita assured her. "My brother called the doctor early this morning to check on her. In fact, he was able to speak with her, too, and she insisted that we let you sleep in. She said she was feeling much better."

Again, Rick Santana seemed to be on top of things, Dallas reflected wryly.

"Why not meet me in the coffee shop?" Anita suggested.

"Okay. I'll be down in twenty minutes or so." Dallas returned the phone to its cradle, pushed her covers aside and slipped from the bed. She crossed on bare-feet to the drapes and pulled a cord to part them, revealing another sun-drenched Spanish morning. She surveyed the broad boulevard below, lined with lofty palms and teeming with traffic. Suddenly she was caught up in the excitement of being in a famous, exotic city. It was, after all, the setting for *Carmen, Don Giovanni*, and *The Barber of Seville*, some of the greatest operas of all time. If she had to be here for a week or more, why not make the most of it? According to Eula's guidebook, there was a lot to see and do.

It wouldn't be hard to find interesting things to occupy her time between visits to the hospital.

As she dressed, Dallas wondered what Rick Santana was up to that morning. She had been surprised and pleased to learn from Anita that he had checked on Eula. As she applied a modest amount of makeup, memories of the previous night made her curiously warm all over. Involuntarily, she found herself hoping that Rick would be in the coffee shop when she joined his sister there. Maybe he was right—Dallas *was* a little afraid of him. He was much too flagrantly masculine for her peace of mind.

When she joined Anita in the restaurant shortly after ten-thirty, Dallas felt a nagging twinge of disappointment. Rick was not there.

"You certainly seem greatly improved over last night," Anita remarked, taking in Dallas's attire, a sleeveless sky-blue cotton dress. It had a Mandarin collar and was belted at her slender waist.

"I must have looked awful." Dallas made a face.

"Oh, I wouldn't go that far." Anita paused to sip at her coffee.

"I want to thank you again for letting me stay here," Dallas told her. "It's so kind of you—and your brother—and the room is absolutely gorgeous. I'll be spoiled by such luxury." She would have to find another place as soon as possible, Dallas had decided. The Palacio Moro was among the most expensive hotels in Seville, and she just didn't feel right about being there when she couldn't really afford even the lowest-price room.

"Spoiled?" Anita echoed. "And why not? I'm a firm believer in the good life. You know, I'd quit working in a minute if the right guy made it worth my while."

Dallas instantly perceived the Spanish girl's bittersweet smile. "But you have such a good job here at the hotel."

Anita nodded. "That's true. It is an excellent position, and I do love my work. But I would like to have a family before it's too late."

"It sounds as if you already have someone in mind," Dallas prompted.

"In my mind and in my heart," came the sober admission.

"Want to tell me about it?" This was all the invitation Anita needed, for she immediately launched into an emotional recital.

"Oh, Dallas, sometimes I feel like I'm just spinning my wheels, but I'm crazy about him." Anita's pretty golden face looked momentarily tormented.

"Him who?"

"Antonio Baez—my boss. The very responsible and efficient manager of the Palacio Moro." Anita grimaced dismally.

Dallas gave a sympathetic smile. "Hmm, I can see where it would be really difficult to work for him feeling that way . . . especially if he doesn't reciprocate."

"Sometimes I suspect that Tony does care—maybe he even loves me—but it would take a miracle to make him admit it."

"How come?" Dallas queried.

"For one thing, Señor Baez believes that you never mix business with . . . well, with one's personal life. He doesn't allow any fraternizing among the staff. Why, just yesterday we had a huge fight because he wanted me to fire one of the maids who's involved with one of our male employees."

"Wow. What happened?" Dallas found herself fascinated by this behind-the-scenes glimpse of the hotel industry.

"I told Antonio that it wasn't a crime to be in love, and if he insisted on firing the girl, the boy must go, too. He got furious, saying that Pablo was one of his best workers, and under no circumstances would he dismiss him. We argued for at least twenty minutes." Anita's gaze remained unhappily colored with that painful memory. "I can tell you, Dallas, a Spanish man does not take kindly to having his decisions questioned by a woman."

"So did he fire the girl?"

"No. I finally told him that if he did, I would resign. He got even angrier, but I was dead serious, and he knew it." Tears suddenly welled in Anita's eyes, and she dabbed at them with her napkin. "What really hurt was Antonio's parting shot," she declared, sniffing loudly. "He said he was disappointed that I would threaten him with quitting, and that I knew he had no choice but to give in to me, since Rick owns the hotel and wouldn't appreciate my resigning over such a trivial matter—as he called it." She sighed. "Which brings us to what I think is the real reason Antonio keeps me at arm's length."

"Because of your brother?" Dallas could certainly appreciate anyone being intimidated by him.

"Exactly," Anita confirmed. "You see, Rick and Antonio met in Madrid after college. Rick studied architecture in the States. Tony attended university in the north . . . in Salamanca. He was from a poor farming area, but he's smart and worked hard and was able to win a government scholarship. Three years ago Rick persuaded him to leave his job in Madrid and move down here to run the hotel. My brother knew Tony would be a great manager, and he really is, believe me. He's just terribly proud and somewhat old-fashioned.

"He wasn't at all happy when Rick asked him to interview me about a year later for the position of assistant manager," Anita confided. "I think he was prepared to resign then, but Rick convinced him it wasn't a family deal. If Tony felt that I couldn't handle the job, or if I botched it, he would be free to let me go with no recriminations from big brother."

"I'll bet you showed both of them a thing or two," Dallas interposed with a grin, causing Anita to giggle. Her tears had dried and were already forgotten.

"Well, I had four years of hotel experience under my belt from working in New York, and I'm pretty good at this business, if I do say so myself."

"So Tony agreed to take you on?"

"Yes, but I got the feeling he only did it out of loyalty to Rick." Anita sighed. "I also think Tony would consider it a major violation of their friendship to even consider getting romantically involved with me."

"Why, for goodness sake?" Dallas exclaimed.

"Oh, Tony has this idiotic notion about social inferiority that's common in Latin countries. You know, the old thing about not wandering from your own class. Heaven knows, he's just as good as we are. So what if his family was poor? As far as I'm concerned, he's a self-made man, just like my father was. I really admire that, and I'd love Tony for it . . . if he'd only let me."

Dallas's brain was clicking away as she listened intently to Anita's story. If this Antonio person really did care for her, surely Rick could be called upon to intervene on his sister's behalf. "Does your brother know how you feel?" she inquired hopefully.

"No indeed!" Anita vehemently shook her head. "I could never tell him. That would ruin everything."

"But maybe he could help you out."

"Dallas, Rick is your typical big brother. He's never really approved of anybody I've been interested in. Just to give you an idea . . . when I was nineteen, I got involved with an American boy from Boston. Rick broke it up in his usual dictatorial fashion. At the time I was crushed—and livid, of course—but later I realized that Rick was right. I was too young to know what I wanted, and Michael was lazy and overly impressed with our wealth. Not to say that he wasn't attracted to me, and probably even loved me in his own way. But I know now we would never have made it together."

Anita raised both hands in an appealing gesture. "You can see why I don't want Rick to know, Dallas. Sure, he respects Tony, and he thinks he's doing a super job for the hotel, but I honestly can't predict how Rick would react if I admitted my feelings." She gave a short, nervous laugh. "Knowing him, he might try to ship me back to Mom in New York." She paused, adding, "And another thing—I would have a hard time forgiving Rick if he said Tony wasn't good enough for me."

"I can't believe your brother would do anything to deliberately hurt you," Dallas blurted impulsively. She shrank back in her chair, shocked by the certainty in her own voice. What was she saying?! She'd only met the man yesterday, and he'd succeeded in making her a nervous wreck. Now she was offering herself as a character witness—to his sister, no less!

"Rick would never believe he was hurting me," Anita replied. "As in the past, he would be doing it for my own good." She smiled ruefully. "Curse him for usually being right. No, Dallas, I have to be very careful. If Rick ever found out that I've fallen for Tony, there wouldn't be any hope for us, I'm positive."

Dallas pondered this while buttering a cold piece of toast. She liked Anita, but she couldn't really empathize with the situation. Being an only child, she found it difficult to understand why a sibling—even an older, commanding male—could exert such an influence over one's life. Then she mentally admonished herself when she remembered that this was, after all, a different culture. In some areas of Spain, she recalled reading, young women were still required to be chaperoned during courtship.

"Now, enough talk about me and my problems, hmm?" Anita grimaced, then smiled. "Do you have anyone serious back in Texas?"

"No . . . I don't," Dallas responded, feeling curiously bereft. "I guess I haven't had much time to get involved." She briefly related her music background and career goals while Anita finished her *café con leche* and popped the last crumb of a sweet roll into her mouth.

"How wonderful to be so talented," Anita chimed. "I'm not crazy about classical music, you understand, but now I'm dying to hear you sing."

Dallas's reply was halted by a cool male voice. "This must be our special guest from the States." She looked up to see an attractive young Spaniard.

"Oh, hi, Tony . . . please meet Miss Dallas Jones from Texas. Dallas, this is my boss, Antonio Baez."

"Encantado, señorita."

Dallas was instantly aware of the tension in the air as her smiling glance shifted from Anita to the hotel manager. She guessed he was still miffed about yesterday's argument. "Won't you join us?" Dallas invited, indicating a vacant chair.

"I wish I could, *señorita*, but I have a lot of work to do." His heavily accented voice was courteous without being warm. A good deal shorter than Rick, but then most Spaniards were, his close-cropped hair was wavy and jet-black, his eyes dark brown. He was certainly handsome, with a healthy olive complexion, and Dallas could appreciate Anita's attraction to him.

"That's his way of telling me to get back to work, Dallas." Anita flashed a sheepish grin and rose reluctantly from the table.

"Not at all, Anita. Take your time," her boss said curtly.

"Still mad about Rosa, eh, Tony?" Anita wasn't going to endure his unreasonable temper, even if she was secretly in love with him.

For a few long seconds they stood arguing in low, heated Spanish tones. Dallas looked on with anxious eyes, wondering if she should exit silently and leave them to their problems. When she started to rise, Anita broke off and turned to her.

"Please excuse our bad manners, Dallas, but you wouldn't find Señor Baez's comments enlightening in any language, so you needn't feel left out."

Antonio's eyes narrowed to black slits. Muttering a hoarse "*Hasta luego*," he turned on his heel and moved quickly in the direction of the lobby. When he was out of sight, Anita collapsed into her chair opposite Dallas and hissed in exasperation. "Oooo, that man! Sometimes I don't know whether to love him or hate him."

"You two really do have a volatile relationship," Dallas observed sympathetically.

"Honestly, this level of arguing is rare for us," Anita assured her. "Tony really is an excellent boss, and I usually agree with his decisions. If you asked him, he

would probably say I'm doing a good job as well."
She sighed. "Yes, we normally make an ideal team.
Unfortunately, there's another type of partnership I'm
interested in. . . ." She and Dallas chuckled in unison.

A moment later Anita glanced down at her watch,
a gleaming gold Rolex. "Oops. I really do need to run.
But hey, I've got the afternoon off—at around four.
The stores reopen then. How would you like to go
shopping for a few hours?"

"I'd love it," Dallas said with a smile. "Just tell me
how to get to the hospital, and I'll meet you back here
around four-thirty."

Chapter Three

During the short ride to the hospital, Dallas's thoughts remained fixed on the fascinating brother and sister occupying the Palacio Moro. From Anita she learned that their father, a successful contractor, had died seven years earlier. Their mother, an American, had remarried and now resided in New York with her stockbroker husband. Dallas had been grateful for this information, because it satisfied her curiosity concerning the Santanas' fluent command of English.

The hotel driver deposited her at Santa Cecilia's front entrance. Minutes later, after stopping several nurses to ask directions, Dallas located Eula's room. She quietly eased the door open and peered inside, surprised to hear the sound of her aunt's pleasant laughter.

"Well, well, doctor . . . it seems you now owe me *five* dollars." From her upright position in bed, Eula was smiling mischievously at the physician who sat opposite her in a straight-back chair.

Roberto Hidalgo retrieved the playing cards strewn on the edge of the bed and shuffled them, chuckling with amusement. "You are a most formidable opponent, *señora*," he said. "May I ask where you learned to play gin with such skill?"

"If my memory serves, it was one of my nephews who taught me a few years ago. Of course, I rarely have the time to play cards."

"Don't you believe a word she says, Dr. Hidalgo." Dallas strolled into the room, interrupting them. "My aunt plays cards with the gals back home at least twice a week."

"Dallas, hon! How are you this morning?" Eula smiled with delight.

Roberto rose and moved his chair to allow Dallas to approach the bed.

"I'm just fine, Auntie." She leaned forward to kiss the woman, carefully avoiding the bandaged leg. "What about you? You're the family casualty."

"Dr. Hidalgo is taking wonderfully good care of me, as you can see."

"Your aunt and I have discovered a mutual interest in gambling," Roberto inserted with a smile. "Fortunately for me, we agreed on a five dollar limit."

"I suggest you beware, doctor. When Aunt Eula starts a card game, it's difficult to get her to stop."

"Have no fear, *señorita*. I am her doctor, and she has little choice but to obey me."

Eula's small hazel eyes twinkled merrily as she rested against several large white pillows at her back. "Dall, sweetie, didn't I tell you I had heard tales of these masterful Spanish men before we left home?"

"Yes, you did mention that," Dallas replied with a grin. "And I'm certainly glad Dr. Hidalgo is keeping an eye on you. We don't want to take any chances with your injuries."

"Well, I'm already feeling one hundred percent better."

"I must be going, ladies. Please excuse me." Roberto nodded politely to Dallas, then turned to Eula, saying, "I will check on you again after lunch, *señora*. Perhaps I can—how do you say?—recoup my losses?" He smiled benevolently, then departed.

"What a dear man," Eula chirped as the door closed behind him.

"Yes, he's very nice. How lucky for us that Rick brought you here."

"Speaking of whom," Eula said, "that was awfully thoughtful of Rick to call this morning, and to look after you, too." She paused pensively. "I must think of some way to repay that young man."

"Why don't you let me worry about him, Aunt. You just concentrate on getting back on your feet again."

"I will do that, of course, Dall, but I can't help but feel very grateful to him. If I had to worry about you all alone in a strange city with me stuck here in the hospital, I'd be absolutely frantic. Rick promised me you would be safe and sound at the hotel."

"Give me a break, Aunt Eula," Dallas retorted, mildly indignant. "I *am* an adult, you know, and I'm quite capable of looking after myself—even in a foreign country."

"I know you are, sweetie, but isn't it nice to have a man watching out for you? And such an attractive one at that!" Eula's eyes were twinkling once again.

"He's okay, I guess," Dallas murmured.

The hours spent at the hospital passed quickly, and Dallas arrived back at the hotel shortly after four o'clock. She was returning to her room to freshen up when she rounded a corner and bumped headlong into Rick in the second floor hallway.

"Oh! Excuse me," she gasped.

Rick's fingers curled around her upper arms to steady her. His smiling gaze skimmed down her blue cotton dress and up again until his focus rested finally on her flushed features.

"Where are you going in such a hurry, *chica*?"

"I have to meet Anita in a few minutes," Dallas replied breathlessly, "and I want to change my shoes. We're going shopping."

"Did you just come from the hospital?" he inquired, removing his hands from her arms and stuffing them casually into the pockets of his charcoal dress slacks.

"Yes." Dallas stared up at him, renewing her original impression of his striking male features. His short straight hair was brushed back from a tanned forehead, and the summer suit jacket he wore over a white linen shirt was the same shade as his smoky eyes. He wasn't wearing a tie, and a patch of thick black hair was visible above the second button of his shirt.

"How is Mrs. Weber doing?" Rick wanted to know.

"She seems to be getting along just fine. She didn't complain of any discomfort while I was there, and she and Dr. Hidalgo have really hit it off." Dallas's cheeks dimpled.

"Roberto is an excellent doctor and a good friend. He and my father grew up together in a small village on the outskirts of Seville."

"Well, Aunt Eula is certainly enjoying his attention. They were playing cards in her room when I arrived this morning."

Rick's inky brows furrowed into a half frown. "I hope she doesn't start getting any ideas where Roberto is concerned."

"What are you talking about?" Now Dallas was frowning.

"He's been a widower for several years now—his wife died of cancer—and he finally seems to have adjusted to the loss. I wouldn't want him to get hurt because of your aunt's flirtations."

Dallas's eyes flared fiery blue in astonishment. "For your information, my aunt is *not* a flirt," she retorted, "and I doubt seriously that anyone could take Uncle Sam's place in her heart."

"There's no need to get defensive," Rick reproved lightly. "As you yourself pointed out yesterday, I believe your exact words were: 'I don't know you from Adam.' Well, I could say the same thing about your aunt. For all I know, she could be a gold-digger on the prowl for a rich husband." He didn't seem to notice the amazed widening of Dallas's gaze. Smiling, he took her hand, saying, "Come with me for a minute, hmm? I'd like to show you something in my office."

Stunned beyond belief that the man could be so utterly insensitive, Dallas allowed herself to be pulled down the long carpeted hallway. The thirty seconds or so it took to reach the hotel's executive suite was just enough time for her resentment to evolve into fuming anger. "I really don't have time to visit your office," she snapped, yanking her hand from his warm grasp. "I'm already late for meeting your sister downstairs."

"Anita can wait a few minutes," Rick clipped dismissively. He swung wide the door and urged Dallas inside. A deserted reception area featuring a computer atop a secretarial desk fronted his spacious office. Dallas was not surprised to see his office fitted with an architect's drawing table in addition to a mammoth oak desk, floor to ceiling bookshelves lining two walls, and a wide picture window overlooking the lush, colorful gardens below.

Rick shut the door behind him and crossed to the desk. Her temper smoldering still, Dallas dropped her purse into a chair and began to pace the thick carpet at her sandaled feet. She wondered what he was rummaging for on top of his messy desk.

"Ah, here it is," he said at last. He turned to her, a large buff-colored card in one hand. "Anita told me about your musical background. As it so happens, I recently completed work on a new theater for our local symphony and opera company. We're hosting a reception here at the hotel on Friday night to celebrate the company's upcoming premiere performance in the new theater."

Dallas stopped pacing. "What's this?" she asked, when he handed her the card.

"An invitation to the reception. You'll enjoy meeting all those music-types," he said magnanimously, taking her acceptance for granted.

"Thank you . . . but I'm afraid the language barrier would sort of leave me out." Her tone was decidedly cool.

"Most members of the company speak at least a little English," Rick countered. "Some of the principals are quite fluent."

Dallas glanced at the card, noted the elegant gold script, and arrived at the perfect excuse to toss his invitation right back in his arrogant face. "I really don't think so," she said with artificial politeness. "It's obviously going to be a very formal affair, and I don't have the proper clothes with me."

"Anita can lend you something," Rick suggested, exasperation lacing his deep voice.

"I couldn't do that—"

"You mean you *won't*," he interrupted her. His annoyed gaze swept her face. "Don't tell me you're still upset because of what I said about your aunt and Roberto?"

Dallas glared up at him with the full force of her

resentment. "You're darn right I am," she declared. "You know, if you're so concerned about the kind of people you and your friends associate with, why did you trouble yourself to help us in the first place?"

"You want the truth?" he asked in a low velvety tone, his frown vanishing.

"Of course," Dallas retorted impulsively, without thinking that she might not really want to hear it. This idea dawned, however, a moment later when Rick stepped forward. His hand lifted, then his lean fingers were moving caressingly down the pale curtain of her hair. His narrowed gaze leisurely appraised her wary features. Alarm rioted within her, but Dallas was incapable of movement, her feet suddenly frozen to the carpet.

"The color is very unusual, almost nonexistent in this part of the world," he murmured, slowly forking his fingers through the thick golden strands that hung to her shoulders. "It caught my attention as I was passing the scene of the accident." When his fingertips brushed her ear, Dallas shivered, but she was still unable to activate her limbs. His warm, affecting touch migrated to her flushed cheek. It glided down to her mouth, and his thumb lingeringly outlined the sensitive curve of her bottom lip.

Every bone in Dallas's body was now threatening to melt like thawing ice. She sucked in her breath, her eyelashes fluttering like the wings of a bird desperate to escape. "I—I know what you're trying to do," she charged in a quavering voice. Ordering her legs into reverse gear, she attempted to back away from him, but was halted by the edge of his massive desk.

"Is that so?" Rick murmured. His hand continued its disturbing path across her jaw, then down the satiny length of her throat. His fingers slid under her hair to cradle her nape, then his thumb pressed gently against the frantically beating pulse in her neck.

"That silly game won't work this time," Dallas rasped, her breathing seriously hampered when Rick casually pulled her closer. What little strength she had remaining, which might have enabled her to draw away, deserted her in an instant.

"What game do you mean, *pequeña?*" With tender insistence, Rick forced her wide-eyed gaze from its mesmerized study of his chest.

"You know—you're just trying to—to intimidate me with that—that macho routine," she accused in a stutter.

Rick chuckled softly as both of his arms encircled her. "Intimidate you into submission, maybe," he agreed. "My sister tells me you're not seriously involved with anyone back in Texas." His intense gaze held her startled eyes. *So he and Anita had been discussing more about me than my music background!* "I find it hard to believe that you're still unattached," he murmured with a wondering smile. "Not only are you intelligent, spirited, and apparently very talented . . . you're also incredibly beautiful."

This shocked Dallas more than anything he'd said thus far. She had been described with many adjectives throughout her life—attractive, cute, pretty—but she couldn't recall anyone ever referring to her as "beautiful," unless they happened to be talking about her singing voice. It was a heady compliment that totally overwhelmed her. Her pulses trilled with the excitement of conflicting emotions. Her innocent gaze dipped involuntarily from his simmering smoky eyes to that firmly chiseled mouth. One part of her wanted him to kiss her more than anything in the world but her self-protective instinct made her frightened of his devastating effect on her.

"I can only conclude that the men in Texas must all be blind . . . or at the very least not too bright," Rick said in a husky voice. His dark head descended and his mouth moved lightly over her lips. She had been kissed before—on stage and for real—but nothing in the past compared to the waves of sensation Rick was generating with his patent expertise.

Dreamily, she melted against him, her hands unconsciously migrating up and around his neck for anchorage.

"Still feeling intimidated?" Rick whispered against her forehead, his arms unwilling to release her.

"Terrified" was the response that came to her mind, but she couldn't admit that to him. Everything was wrong about this—the time, the place, the man. Dallas didn't need or want an emotional involvement at this point in her young life, and encouraging someone like Rick Santana could be a risky—even dangerous—proposition. Obviously, he had a lot of experience with women. No doubt his interest in her meant nothing more than a fleeting summer romance to him.

Well, it just wasn't acceptable to her serious nature to indulge in casual short-lived relationships. Besides, her career had been her focus for as long as she could remember. Several men had tried before to veer her from that chosen path. Each of them had failed . . . only none had been as bold as this one.

"Rick . . . please," she stammered, "I—I really do have to go."

"Not yet, *chica*, hmm?" he murmured, inhaling the floral fragrance of her skin. "What perfume are you wearing?" he demanded softly. "It's so subtle, but alluring all the same. I don't think I've ever smelled it before." Dallas's shallow breathing made it difficult to respond. Her legs seemed completely weightless, and her head spun dizzily, in the same debilitating way it had the day before . . . only this was definitely not related to the blow received in the accident. She wanted to resist him, or at least she knew she should, but she couldn't seem to find the strength to draw away from him.

"It—it's *Destiny*," Dallas managed at last, her voice timorous and low.

"What's destiny?" Rick lifted his head. He smiled curiously down into her dazed eyes.

"That's the name . . . of my perfume," she explained shakily, affected by the glitter in the sooty depths of his eyes. "You asked me the name of it . . ."

He chuckled quietly. "Oh, right . . . I thought maybe you were trying to tell me it's destiny for us to be together." He framed her face with his hands, his fingers stroking her silky eyebrows and flushed cheeks.

"Rick, you have to stop . . . *now*," Dallas insisted, rendered horribly vulnerable by his words as well as by his relentless touch. It took a tremendous effort, but she planted her hands on his chest and shoved. His shoulders barely moved, but his head lifted. "Something wrong?" he teased her in a husky tone.

"I told you . . . I really do have to go." She tried valiantly to sound emphatic, even though the desire to stay within the heated circle of his embrace was overpowering.

Rick seemed to ponder her words, while his smoking gaze unhurriedly perused her soft lips. His arms slackened fractionally when he heaved a sigh, as if he were resigned to the truth of her statement. "I suppose you must," he agreed with obvious reluctance. "All right . . . give me your promise that you'll attend the party on Friday night, and then I'll let you go."

Dallas was not above breaking her word when it was procured in such a questionable manner, so she responded at once. "I promise," she said in a small voice.

"Hey, that was much too easy," Rick drawled, eyeing her suspiciously. "We'd better make the penalty a heavy one, so you don't get any ideas about backing out."

"I'll be there . . . I will," she assured him quickly.

"Be very sure that you are, *mujer*, or I'll be forced to track you down."

Like a lion chasing a scared rabbit, she reflected grimly, wondering why he was so determined that she attend the reception. Mentally she concluded that Rick

Santana was simply in the habit of bending people to his will, as in the case of his younger sister.

"Muy bueno," Rick said softly. "Now . . . to seal the promise, hmm?" Dallas watched a brief smile touch his handsome face. Then his head bent, and he covered her lips in a final kiss. It lasted only a matter of seconds, but jolted her like a surge of electricity, leaving her giddy and weak.

Later, she was at a complete loss as to how she had remembered to retrieve her purse and successfully retrace her steps out of his office, through the door and down the hallway until she reached the secure haven of her room. Her legs threatened to buckle beneath her, her mind was muddled and disoriented, and her galloping heart was giving her severe chest pains.

Chapter Four

During their first outing together, Dallas and Anita discovered a mutual love of shopping. Consequently, they wasted no time scheduling another expedition to the city's bustling center only two days later.

Calle Sierpes in the heart of Seville was a quaint cobblestone street lined with shops, boasting everything from fine gold jewelry to the lovely porcelain figurines coveted by many travelers visiting the Iberian Peninsula.

Earlier in the trip, Dallas and Eula had conversed at length over which pieces of Lladró they would splurge on as souvenirs of Spain. Lladró porcelain, beautiful damascene jewelry from Toledo, and colorful hand-painted flamenco fans were immensely popular with the tourist trade.

"I know Aunt Eula wanted a nativity set," Dallas told Anita as they strolled along Calle Sierpes.

"Casa Esmeralda has a good selection, and their prices are reasonable," Anita said. "It's located in the next block. Let's look there."

Dallas wanted to surprise Eula with a gift. When she'd visited the hospital that morning, she'd found her aunt discouraged and somewhat depressed over the prospect of a prolonged recuperation period. The doctor's original prognosis of several days had been extended due to the onset of a low-grade temperature. To Eula's disappointment, Roberto had curtailed their friendly card games—until the fever dissipated, he'd said.

Casa Esmeralda's smiling staff greeted the shoppers politely, recognizing Anita, a regular customer, immediately. For over an hour, Dallas surveyed shelf after shelf of delicately crafted figurines, expertly hand-painted in shades of pink, blue, green, yellow, gray and taupe. At one point her attention was drawn to a piece she hadn't seen in any of the shops she and Eula had visited in Madrid—an adorable seven-inch tall figure of a bride and groom.

Anita noticed her interest. "Don't you love it?" the Spanish girl exclaimed. "For a while now I've been tempted to add that one to my collection, but I'm afraid of putting a hex on 'you know what'!" Her short laugh had a rueful edge to it.

"Don't be so superstitious," Dallas said with a smile. "Why not get it? It is a beauty."

"I really should, hmm? Wouldn't it look just peachy on top of a wedding cake?"

"A very large one," Dallas agreed.

The detail on the piece was impressive. Finely-etched lace adorned the bride's gown, and tiny individual flowers studded her bouquet. The groom carried gray gloves and a top hat. A single white carnation perched on the lapel of his suit.

Anita sighed and shook her head. "No, I can't bring myself to buy it yet. If I ever succeed in breaking through Tony's defenses, I'll definitely treat myself."

Dallas eventually decided on a three-piece nativity set for Eula, a stately Don Quixote for her mother, and a fairy-sized ballerina for her roommate, Joanie. For herself Dallas chose a little gypsy girl cradling a basket of oranges in her arms. A cute white kitten rested at her feet.

It was dusk when they emerged from the shop. Within minutes Anita had hailed a taxi, and they were loading armfuls of parcels onto the narrow backseat.

"El Palacio Moro, por favor," Anita instructed the driver. Then, with a giggle bubbling from her curving lips, she turned to Dallas. "If the guys could see us now! Nothing like an afternoon of retail therapy to lift your spirits, right?"

"It works for me," Dallas agreed, her thoughts immediately turning to one of "the guys" to whom she knew Anita had referred.

"Oh, by the way, Rick wants us to meet him in the Torre del Oro Restaurant at nine," Anita said.

"I thought you said he left for Barcelona on business the day before yesterday," Dallas rejoined in surprise.

"He got back this afternoon," Anita replied, her voice lilting with sudden excitement. "He said he was going to ask Tony to dine with us tonight."

"I take it you don't often get the chance to mix socially with your boss." Dallas tried to sound nonchalant, even though her pulse was scurrying with alarm and something else. The thought of being with Rick again triggered those conflicting feelings of hers. Whenever she relived that interlude in his office, her face burned and her heartbeat accelerated disturbingly. She wanted to see him, but at the same time she was afraid of his effect on her emotions.

"Tony and I occasionally entertain clients together," Anita explained, "but he's always so terribly businesslike. I was kind of surprised when Rick suggested that the four of us have dinner together."

"Maybe your brother suspects something and is trying to help you out," Dallas said.

"No way!" Anita gave a mirthless little grunt. "I'm sorry, Dallas, but I can't picture Rick in the role of matchmaker." Then, green eyes gleaming with sudden speculation, she shifted to study her new friend's face. "I wonder if my dear workaholic brother has finally wised up and decided on a bit of a social life himself." She flashed an impish grin. "I wouldn't blame him . . . seeing how very pretty and talented our special guest is."

Warm color flooded Dallas's cheeks as she gave a

quick shake of her head. "Forget it, Anita. It's obvious your brother and I aren't in the same league."

"Really? I'm sorry to hear that." The attractive brunette appeared genuinely disappointed. "Well, I guess I've always known that Rick will never fall for an American girl. Our mom is from the States, but Rick's Spanish genes are definitely the more dominant. If and when he bothers to settle down, he's bound to choose a woman from over here." She chuckled. "Besides, what modern American female would put up with his domineering ways? He's all male, that one."

She could say that again, Dallas thought, grimacing inwardly.

"Getting back to dinner tonight," Anita chattered on, "Rick probably just wants to talk business with Tony and me, and maybe he thought you could use some company. Whatever the reason, I'm counting my blessings and searching my wardrobe. I plan to look positively stunning this evening, preferably in something Señor Antonio Baez has never seen me in before. It's my latest strategy."

Dallas couldn't help but smile in response to Anita's chirpy mood. "Aren't you overlooking 'the way to a man's heart is through his stomach' routine?" she queried, dimpling.

"Ha! And try to compete with the chefs at the hotel? I wouldn't have a prayer, *amiga*. I'm afraid my looks and sparkling wit will have to see me through this . . . and your support, of course." Anita grinned, then she became serious. "Honestly, Dallas, I'm so glad you're here. It's terrific to have someone to confide in. I guess

I've been so involved with my job these last few years, I haven't had a lot of time to make any close friends."

Still plagued by indecision where Rick was concerned, Dallas hesitated. "I don't want to seem antisocial, but I think I'd better stick to room service tonight. I'm really tired, and I have to be at the hospital early tomorrow morning." She avoided her companion's searching eyes. "Besides, I'm still not used to your Spanish dinner hours. I'm famished now, and it's only seven."

"You'll just have to have a snack and rest for an hour or so before we go." Anita's voice was emphatic. "I refuse to take 'no' for an answer, and neither would Rick, I promise you."

"But—"

"No 'buts' either," Anita chided, wagging a red-tipped finger in Dallas's face. "I'll be at your door at nine sharp to take you up to the restaurant." Anita smiled in happy anticipation. "You'll love it, really. We're all very proud of the Torre del Oro. It's named after the historic Tower of Gold, the centuries-old landmark on the Guadalquivir River."

"But it sounds so elegant," Dallas persisted, still fishing for an excuse, "and I'm not sure I have an appropriate outfit."

"Any dress will do, silly. And if you don't want to wear something of yours, I have dozens of things you're more than welcome to try."

"I'll manage, I suppose." Dallas sighed.

"It's settled then, hmm? No more excuses." Anita's eyes twinkled teasingly as the taxi swerved and braked at the hotel entrance. "One would think you were averse to our company, *amiga*. Believe me, Rick and Tony can be quite charming when they're behaving themselves." Anita paused pensively, then she grinned. "Maybe the problem is you've never seen them when they *were* behaving."

"I'll say," Dallas muttered under her breath as she was helped from the car by a smiling doorman.

Even at nine o'clock, the beginning of the Spanish dinner hour, the Torre del Oro Restaurant was pulsating with energy. Dallas and Anita entered together, the latter attired in a shimmering magenta sheath. The scalloped neckline revealed the barest hint of cleavage, and the hem met the bottom of her knees.

"Wow! If Antonio doesn't notice you in that," Dallas had commented moments before, "he isn't alive."

Anita had reciprocated in kind, gushing over her friend's sleeveless floral print dress with its soft sarong-like skirt touching the middle of her calves. The deep jewel tones were a flattering contrast to her blond hair, which she'd pulled back from her face with decorative combs. Tiny clusters of pink sapphires, set in yellow gold, dangled from her delicate earlobes. The earrings were a gift from her grandparents, who'd gotten them on a recent trip to Hong Kong.

Beneath the romantic lighting of luminous chandeliers, the Torre del Oro unfolded as a maze of white-clothed tables topped with glimmering silver flatware, ivory china and sparkling crystal goblets. Patrons conversed sedately in a dozen different languages, many totally foreign to Dallas, as she and Anita threaded their way to a secluded table.

Her pulse skipping in anticipation, Dallas found herself rather short of breath when they reached Antonio Baez and Rick. Both men stood instantly, looking darkly attractive in European-cut suits with starched shirts and silk designer ties.

"Don't you two *caballeros* look devilishly handsome this evening," Anita greeted them gaily.

Even though Rick didn't verbally return the compliment, his appreciative glance told both females he approved their attire.

"*Señorita . . . aquí, por favor.*" He whipped a chair back from the table and murmured for Dallas to sit at his right. She shyly returned his smile with a polite "*gracias.*"

"Aren't you going to hold my chair, Tony?" Anita queried.

Dallas glanced up to notice Antonio staring speechlessly at his assistant manager. "Oh, *sí-sí,*" the young man stuttered, considerably flustered.

When everyone was seated, Anita addressed her brother. "How did your meeting with Jorge Montalvo go?"

"It went very well. We should be ready to begin work on their new building next month." Rick paused with an explanation for Dallas. "Montalvo Industries asked me to design a new administrative office for them in Barcelona. They're one of the largest employers in Spain, with offices in several cities, including Seville. Jorge and his wife live here."

"And how is Cora?" Anita inquired.

"Not very happy at the moment, I'm afraid," Rick replied. "Jorge told me that her jewelry was stolen Saturday night while they were attending a concert."

"How awful!" Anita and Dallas chorused.

"Was it the work of a professional?" Antonio leaned forward, his dark eyes narrowed with interest.

"The police seem to think so. Jorge had a well-concealed wall safe installed in their home years ago. The thief or thieves had no trouble finding it and getting inside. Cora's collection is worth a small fortune, and no one is offering much hope of recovering any of it."

"A pity," Antonio said. "Had he insurance?"

"Sure . . . but Cora will not be consoled according to Jorge. You know how these women are," Rick drawled, flicking an indolently indulgent gaze over the two gracing his table. "They attach sentimental value to such things." His glance lighted on his sister. "Remember the jeweled brooch Jorge gave to Cora for their tenth anniversary last year?"

"Indeed I do," Anita recalled. "It was lovely—a gold butterfly covered with diamonds, rubies and emeralds."

"Not that expensive compared to a lot of her pieces," Rick pointed out, "but apparently Cora is still crying over it." He shook his head as if that were totally beyond his comprehension.

"Poor girl," Anita exclaimed. Then she flashed an aggravated look that encompassed the men at the table. "Naturally we would never expect you two to understand how she feels. Neither of you knows a darn thing about women."

Dallas watched the expressions playing over their faces. Rick's mouth split into a broad grin, his white teeth glinting. Antonio appeared puzzled and a trifle indignant. Anita's delicate scowl evolved into an exasperated smile. "Even so, you always manage to make us want you," she admitted candidly, her light-hearted mood restored.

Rick said nothing, but his direct, assessing gaze slid to Dallas's face. Her nerves tensed in response to his lingering regard, intended to remind her of their encounter in his office, she was sure. She felt the warmth of a blush reddening her cheeks, and could have applauded the white-coated waiter who chose that moment to appear.

Rick ordered their meal. Soon they were chatting over courses of delicious *Gazpacho Andaluz*, a spicy chilled soup made of tomato, cucumber, vinegar and olive oil; a steaming rice dish called *Paella Valenciana*; and finally, a thick, tender steak, grilled to perfection. It was served with creamy garlic potatoes, fresh spinach and artichoke hearts. The ever-smiling and efficient waiters were determined to please, in light of these particular patrons. It wasn't often that the Torre del Oro welcomed the hotel's owner, manager, and assistant manager all in one fell swoop!

Following a sweet dessert of peach melba, which the men declined, Rick suggested an after-dinner coffee in the Palacio Moro's top-floor nightclub, the Oasis. Dallas's pupils dilated within moments of entering

the large low-ceilinged cavern. When her vision adjusted to the dim lighting, she saw that the club offered
the same opulent Moorish flavor found throughout the
hotel. There were luxurious velvet couches lining two
adjacent walls and small round tables were shrouded
in red and lit with scented candle lanterns.

A six-piece brass and string combo located beyond
the crowded dance floor was engrossed in a spirited
rendition of a Brazilian samba. Blaring horns glinted
like hammered gold beneath spotlights aimed at the
small elevated stage. A smiling young man was
pounding energetically on a shining black grand piano.

Not unexpectedly, the Santana party was given a
special table away from the tourist throng currently
inhabiting the hotel. The composure Dallas had gained
over dinner evaporated into the smoke-hung atmosphere when she found herself beside Rick on the
cushions of their plush corner sofa. Immediately alert
to his warmth, heating her skin through the fine fabric
of her dress, she sat rigid, her hands clenched in her
lap. Grasping for something to distract her from her
vivid awareness of the man at her side, she trained
her attention on the scene before them—the lively
band, uninhibited dancers, and waiters meandering
around the clusters of small tables.

Anita, situated between Dallas and Antonio, took
full advantage of the tight seating arrangements. The
limited size of their couch provided a welcome intimacy, ideal for her latest strategy. From time to time,
she permitted her lovely stockinged legs to acciden-

tally brush her boss's. She leaned into him frequently, speaking distinctly in his ear, so as to be heard above the musical din of the exotic Oasis.

"Would you please relax," Rick commanded gruffly, inclining his head for a closer inspection of Dallas's shadowed face. She blinked at him through anxious eyes. Seconds later she felt him capture one of her hands. "Your skin is like ice," he murmured, close to her ear. He enfolded her fingers in the warmth of his.

"My hands are always cold," Dallas murmured. When his thumb began an absent massage of her palm, her pulse skittered in reaction.

"What was that? What did you say?" Rick released her hand and his arm came around her shoulders. "It's hard to hear over the music," he complained. A lump rose in Dallas's throat when his face hovered within an inch of hers. Rick's faintly twitching lips were the only giveaway that he was enjoying his effect on her.

Anita was still huddled close to her boss, deep in conversation and oblivious to the other couple. A waiter arrived with coffee. Dallas reached forward to lift her cup from their table, grateful for a reason to escape Rick's disturbing touch. But as soon as she leaned back on their couch, his arm resumed its warm possession of her shoulders. With a resigned grimace, she gave up and relaxed against his side, determined to enjoy the club and the music. Soon she was drifting dreamily along, lulled by the haunting quality of the band's current selection, a softly stirring instrumental.

Her eyes closed and her head comfortably nestled itself against Rick's shoulder.

"You're not falling asleep on me, are you, *chica*?" he demanded. His deep teasing tone awakened her to the moment.

Her lashes flew up and her wide gaze shot to his as she protested: "Of course not . . . I was just enjoying the music. It's a beautiful piece, and I don't believe I've ever heard it before." She looked down and hastily gulped the remainder of her coffee.

"No, I'm sure it wouldn't be a part of your repertoire," he said. "The gypsy music of Andalucía doesn't often stray from this region."

"I wonder why not," Dallas mused thoughtfully. She had performed several Hungarian songs in her junior year at UT that had gypsy origins.

"Perhaps because it personifies the brooding, passionate nature of the Spanish people," Rick rejoined, "something an outsider would have difficulty appreciating or even understanding."

One of the musicians stepped forward, a guitar in his hands, and began to sing, his rich tenor voice filling the now hushed cavern. There was a plaintive, almost anguished quality to his performance. After a dramatically building crescendo, he ended on a loud high note accompanied by a frenzied strumming of his guitar which lasted for several seconds.

There was thunderous applause, and Dallas was delighted when the young man performed two more numbers. At one point, wishing she could understand the words, she asked Rick for a translation.

"They're all romantic ballads, of course," he drawled, an indulgent curve softening his firm lips. "That one tells the story of a pair of star-crossed lovers. The first time the man sees the girl, washing herself by a stream in the forest, he is enchanted by her fair beauty. She belongs to a gypsy caravan, but her long, flowing hair is as golden as the sun, her eyes as clear and blue as the summer sky."

Dallas's heartbeat accelerated as she recalled Rick's comment about her own blond hair, and how it had caught his attention the day of the accident. Now she felt his perceptive gaze on her face. It rattled her, making her think he had read her mind again.

"It doesn't have a happy ending, does it?" she queried inanely, hating the nervousness he always managed to arouse in her.

"Star-crossed lovers in fact or fiction rarely do," he pointed out, grinning gently at her.

"Oh, that's true." She colored, feeling foolish in his eyes.

Following the wonderful gypsy music, the band took up an instrumental arrangement of a popular British soft rock number. Couples began eagerly filing to the deserted dance floor. Rick rose, pulling Dallas to her feet. "May I have this dance, *señorita*?" he asked, bowing.

"*Sí, señor.*" A smile tugged at her lips. He could be such a charming rogue when the mood struck him.

Because of her relaxed state, Dallas's feet felt leaden as she trailed him, her hand in his, to the oval area in front of the stage. The lights had been dimmed to encourage the more timid individuals who might have been tempted to indulge in such a romantic ambiance.

Rick shouldered through several couples. Turning to Dallas he drew her into his arms with a swift, graceful flourish that took her breath away. Her sluggish feet instantly awakened. He held her close, allowing little space between them, the branding imprint of his hand at the small of her back. As they danced, she experienced a ripple of happiness that grew until it touched every nerve ending from her head to her toes.

Fortunately, the innate sense of rhythm that contributed to her musical talent enabled her to follow him admirably, in spite of her fragile composure. But she had to tunnel her concentration on her feet, because the steady beat of his heart was a constant reminder of another occasion when she had been in his arms.

She stiffened when she felt Rick's lips brush against the sensitive shell of her ear. "If you sing as well as you dance, we may have to find a reason to keep you in Seville," he said in a provocative whisper.

Smiling, Dallas inquired: "Was that a job offer, *señor?*" Her fingers relaxed against his lapel where he had cupped them in the warm prison of his hand.

"You know it was a compliment," he said softly. "Why do you act coy, Dallas? You're not the type, and it doesn't fit you."

Mildly irritated, she peered up at him. "What makes you think you know me so well when we just met a few days ago?"

"I know women." A brief smile touched his mouth.

The pressure of his hand at her waist increased slightly when she drew a little away from him.

"Well, you were wrong about Eula," Dallas responded with artificial sweetness, provoked by his judgmental attitude.

Rick sighed. His black brows lifted in exasperation. "I didn't intend to sound like I was expressing a negative opinion of your aunt, and I'm sorry you were offended by my comments."

A young couple jostled Dallas from behind, murmuring apologies when she reflexively turned her head at the intrusion. Rick smoothly maneuvered her to a less congested area. The musicians modulated into another slow number. A husky-voiced girl, who appeared out of the shadows, began to sing a familiar tune from a classic Broadway musical.

"I've always loved that song," Dallas murmured, more to herself than for her partner's hearing.

"Then why don't you hush and enjoy it?" Rick grumbled into her hair. "And please stop trying to pick a fight with me." His arms clenched playfully around her, as if to emphasize her female inferiority, at least in the physical sense. When she stole a resentful glance at his face, she detected a wicked glint in his eyes beneath the club's dim lighting.

With a resigned sigh, she decided to accept his smug advice. Closing her eyes, she let the lilting music fill her mind. Hardly aware that she did so, she melted into Rick, snuggling against his elegantly-clothed shoulder like a trusting kitten. His earlier comment about keeping her in Seville made her contemplate what it might be like to live in Spain. It was an extraordinarily beautiful country, and she found herself rapidly becoming enamored with the exciting and picturesque capital of Andalucía.

Once, when she opened her eyes momentarily during the dance, she spotted Anita and Antonio across the floor, locked together in a similar manner. Anita appeared totally unaware of the other couples encircling them. Dallas wondered if Rick had seen them as well. Could his perceptive eyes fail to notice his sister's interest in her boss as something more than the respect and loyalty of a dedicated employee? Yet men were often obtuse about such things.

The final notes of the song wafted to her ears, and Dallas found herself curiously reluctant to leave the snug haven of Rick's embrace. She had grown used to the feel of his strong jaw against her hair, the subtle musky essence of an expensive cologne, and the incredible cradling warmth of his arms and hands.

"We can stay here all night, *niña*, but I think the musicians are taking a break." Rick's deep voice teased her quietly when she made no move to withdraw. The music had died—at least the band was no longer playing. However, the seductive melody still floated along in Dallas's pleasure-clouded brain.

"Oh!" Hot color seared her face. She took a hasty backward step when Rick's arms fell from around her. His amused smile told her he recognized and appreciated his potent effect on her nervous system. Heart drumming furiously in her breast, Dallas retreated to the couch, distressed that she suddenly felt chilled and bereft without his warm touch.

A long-distance phone call took Rick from the Oasis within minutes of their return to the table. Before he excused himself he turned to speak to Antonio, whom appeared as dazed as she herself was feeling.

"As a precaution, we should alert security and double check the vault's alarm system," Rick clipped. "Jorge said the police mentioned that his was one of several robberies in Seville in the past two weeks."

Antonio snapped to attention at the mere mention of business. "I'll take care of it right away," he promised.

Never one to be left out, Anita chimed in. "I'll instruct the desk crew to encourage every guest to use the safety deposit boxes until the thieves are caught."

"Good idea," Rick agreed. "All we need right now is a rash of room robberies to really stir things up this summer."

Chapter Five

The telephone jangled insistently as Dallas emerged from the bathroom the following morning. She fumbled with the buttons of a seagreen cotton shirtwaist as she reached for the phone.

"*Huevos revueltos* in fifteen minutes," a deep masculine voice announced.

Dallas felt a rush of pleasure mingled with nervousness when she recognized Rick's voice. "*Huevos revueltos* . . . scrambled eggs, hmm? Are you fixin'?" she asked with a slow smile, her hand resting on the final button at her throat.

"Lucky for you, I'm not," Rick retorted wryly. "I'm a lousy cook."

"At least you're honest." Her smile expanded to a

grin as she tried to picture Rick anywhere near a kitchen.

"Right . . . honest and hungry," he growled. "Meet me in the coffee shop in fifteen minutes," he ordered imperiously.

Dallas grimaced. *The man could be an absolute dictator!* Well, she wasn't about to overlook his bossy antics. "I would consider meeting you," she allowed sweetly, "only you forgot to say the magic word."

"*Por favor, señorita*—please," Rick said, his tone amused. He hung up, leaving Dallas to wonder how many women had succumbed to his undeniable attraction. He was probably used to having numerous eager females at his beck and call. Well, she had no intention of becoming one of those conquests, no matter how determined he was to add her to the list. She tried to summon a flicker of resentment toward him, but as she hurried to finish dressing, all she felt was excited anticipation about seeing him again.

Dallas had read somewhere that continental breakfasts were standard fare in Spain, but it was at once obvious that they were not included in the daily rituals of the Palacio Moro's architect owner.

"You just can't beat a real American breakfast," Rick remarked as he and Dallas indulged in large portions of steaming eggs, fried ham, and hot bread covered with rich butter and strawberry preserves.

"That was so good, but much too much for me," she complained.

"Aw, come on . . . have some more," he urged.

Then a lazy grin creased his handsome face. "You could use a few more pounds, you know. Aren't singers supposed to be broad around the middle?" His teasing glance lingeringly appraised her, from neck to waist, causing a blush to steal to the roots of her pale hair.

"I don't know what gave you that idea," Dallas retorted. She inclined her head and pretended to adjust her napkin.

"Those delightfully plump prima donnas I always see performing at the opera, of course," Rick said, his tone and eyes full of mischief. "I just assumed you needed the extra weight to support all those piercing high notes."

Dallas found his light mood warming her into a friendly camaraderie, something so unexpected she felt buoyant with pleasure. "Well, take my word for it, *señor*," she responded primly. "We less-padded sopranos manage to hit those notes with the same degree of success."

"I stand corrected," he said, grinning, and then paused to sip at his black, unsugared coffee.

"So, you've been to the opera?" Dallas probed with curious interest. Except for her fellow music students, most of the younger guys she knew wouldn't be caught dead sitting through an opera.

"You sound surprised," Rick observed, smiling.

"A little," Dallas admitted.

"Why?"

"Let's just say that most men I know would prefer watching a football or baseball game on Saturday night rather than seeing *The Marriage of Figaro* or *Rigoletto* on public television."

"Well, I enjoy Mozart, Verdi *and* football," Rick said casually.

Now Dallas was really astounded—he actually knew the composers of those operas!

They talked of many things over the remainder of breakfast. Rick wanted to know about her father, a university professor, and whether she had any brothers and sisters. When she told him that her mother had a mild heart condition, and had been advised by her doctor not to have any more babies after Dallas's birth, Rick surprised her once again.

"That's too bad," he said. "There's nothing to equal a large family. As close as Anita and I are, I always wished that our mother had wanted more children." His face assumed a pensive, almost brooding look. "She really planned to stop after I came along . . . apparently Anita was an accident."

"How did your father feel?" Dallas queried gently, grateful for the instant smile that transformed Rick's sober face.

"Papá would gladly have had a dozen kids," Rick exclaimed, smiling. "Of course, having been raised a Roman Catholic, he felt morally obligated, but beyond that, he simply loved kids." Rick's expression clouded again. "Once, when Anita and I were in grade school, I overheard my parents in a terrible argument. Funny— I remember it as if it were only yesterday. Mother was yelling in English that she had no intention of raising any more children in this primitive country." Rick sighed heavily. "And poor Papá couldn't understand. They weren't well–off at the time—he had just started a small construction company—but they weren't poor, either."

"Rick, maybe emotionally your mom just couldn't handle more than two children." Dallas added, trying to cheer him, "Especially since you were one of them."

He laughed. "Hey, I wasn't all that bad," he protested, "although Anita would undoubtedly disagree." Then a bitter twist returned to his mouth. "No, my mother's problem always seemed related to a single cause: she just didn't want to live here.. Why in the world she married a Spaniard, I'll never know. She sure managed to make his life miserable most of the time."

"Maybe she found Spain a little . . . uh . . . *backward* in comparison to home," Dallas ventured hesitantly.

Rick met her gaze. "Is that *your* impression so far?"

"No—no, of course not," she assured him. She might just as easily have told him how quickly she had fallen in love with his country. It was a beautiful and intriguing land—as geographically diverse as it was rich in history and culture.

"Listen, Dallas," Rick explained earnestly, "as much as I care for her, I recognized very early that my mother was a selfish, spoiled only child looking for adventure and romance and a ticket out of New Jersey. She was a foolish dreamer with unrealistic expectations of love and marriage, and absolutely no sensitivity to cultural distinctions. I don't think she ever understood that it isn't where you live that's really important; it's the people around you who love you that matter."

"You make her sound so shallow, Rick. Are you sure you're being fair?" Dallas resented his reference to the "only child" stereotype. She herself had carried that label and knew how quick people were to condemn the child for being spoiled and egocentric, yet rarely willing to sympathize with her loneliness. "There are always two sides to any relationship, you know," Dallas went on quickly. "Maybe your mother and father were basically incompatible, and no matter where they lived, they would have had marital problems."

"You could be right," Rick allowed, shrugging his wide shoulders beneath the fawn jacket covering them. "Anyway, that's all in the past. My mother seems content with her second husband and her apartment in New York. And Papá, God rest his soul, despite all their fighting, he adored her to the end."

Later, Dallas pondered Rick's candid disclosure concerning his parents. She wondered if their stormy relationship had made their only son skeptical of marriage. According to Anita, Rick could take his pick of the local *señoritas*, but she had also referred to her brother as a workaholic. Perhaps when he wasn't engrossed in his work, he enjoyed the role of "continental playboy," as Dallas had initially pegged him.

During one of her regular visits to Santa Cecilia, Dallas found that Eula's spirits had lifted markedly.

Roberto Hidalgo had been to see her just prior to her niece's arrival. He'd promised Eula he would return after lunch for a chat and a game of cards.

"Honey, do you think I'm too old to fall in love again?" Eula asked with a pensive smile after her niece was seated in a bedside chair.

Mild shock momentarily registered on Dallas's face. "Aunt Eula, darling, you've only known Dr. Hidalgo for a week," she exclaimed, guessing the obvious. "You can't possibly think you're in love with him." Rick's words echoed relentlessly in her mind. He had pointed out that Roberto was finally adjusted to his widowed state. After five years of living alone since her husband's death, Eula seemed content with her life as well. Dallas hated to think that her aunt might be disappointed and hurt when the time came for them to return to the States.

"Why can't I think I'm in love?" Eula demanded, exhibiting her characteristic spunk. "I knew how I felt about your uncle the moment I saw him." She paused, her restless boney fingers fidgeting with the crisp salt and pepper strands curling around her ear. "Oh, Dall, you're probably right. It's just wishful thinking on my part, I reckon. But ever since Sammy passed away, I've hoped to meet another good man I could learn to love—someone to share the rest of my days with. Somebody strong, but also kind and caring. You know, someone like Roberto—"

"He *is* awfully nice," Dallas allowed, smiling sympathetically. Deciding a change of topic was in order, she told Eula about the reception that evening. "I didn't bring anything with me that would be suitable for such a formal affair," she admitted.

"You get yourself over to a fancy shop as soon as you leave here," Eula ordered, "and buy yourself something pretty." She tried to get Dallas to accept some money to pay for a dress, but her niece stoutly refused.

"You and Rick Santana, Aunt!" Dallas exclaimed, making a face and shaking her head. "If you two had your way, I'd be a charity case for sure. I tried to discuss my bill with a man at the front desk of the hotel this morning, and he acted like I had the plague." Dallas ruefully recalled the scene in her mind. She had argued with the guy for ten minutes, had even whipped out her travelers checks, and was prepared to insist that he take her money when he had begged: "*Señorita, por favor*! If I accept one dollar from you, Señor Santana will fire me for certain. I am quite serious." The poor middle-aged man had broken into a nervous sweat. So she had no choice but to take pity upon him and drop the subject.

Around three-thirty, Eula, hazel eyes blinking thoughtfully, reached for one of the thick paperbacks Dallas had purchased for her in the hotel's gift shop. "Why don't you run along, hon? You've spent enough time sitting with me for one day. Roberto will be checking in soon."

Dallas searched her aunt's round crinkled face, then rose without an argument. "Okay, I think I get the message," she teased the older woman. "You want to be alone with your new beau. Far be it from me to hang around here if I'm not really needed." Her blue eyes twinkled playfully.

"Don't you dare sass me, young lady." Eula issued a mock reprimand. "Hit the road!"

"I'm going, I'm going." Dallas giggled. "I'll see you tomorrow." She kissed Eula's cheek, walked to the door and turned. "Remember, Auntie: don't do anything I wouldn't do." Eula waved her away with a grimace, settled back against her pillows, and pretended to read her book.

Dallas telephoned Anita from the hospital's lobby to discover where she should go to find a dress for the night ahead. The assistant manager insisted that her new friend was more than welcome to use one of her gowns, but Dallas knew the size wouldn't be quite right. Besides, the bold colors Anita favored would certainly overpower Dallas's pale, delicate features.

"Try the Gallerías Preciosas," Anita suggested, when she realized Dallas would not be swayed into borrowing a dress. "It's a very nice department store. They should have something for you. Any taxi can take you there."

Contrary to what Anita had said, the large store had little to offer in the line of evening dresses. But Dallas located a small boutique on the next block with several possibilities in her conservative price range. Eventually she settled on an ultra-feminine modified flamenco creation in a soft dusky rose. The puffed sleeves, rounded neckline and layered fitted skirt were trimmed with fine ecru lace. For long minutes she wondered uncertainly if the dress wasn't too overstated, considering how very Spanish it looked, and how fair her coloring was. It would undoubtedly make her appear to be in costume. *So what if it did?* she finally decided, giving in to her theatrical alter ego. If her coloring made her stick out like a sore thumb anyway, why not make the most of it?

Dallas was pleased with her decision as soon as she tapped lightly on Anita's door. She turned the knob as the voice inside beckoned her to enter. Pausing on the threshold, she laughed merrily at the brunette's shrill whistle of approval.

"You certainly did well, *mi amiga*," Anita exclaimed, stepping forward. "That dress is a knockout. For sure I ought to lock you in your room tonight. I don't need any more competition—"

"Oh, cut it out," Dallas interrupted chidingly. "You know you look gorgeous in that." She gestured to Anita's strapless daffodil-yellow chiffon, its full ankle-length skirt rustling above a pair of sexy gold high-heeled sandals.

"I do look good, don't I?" Anita giggled. "Well, I'd better, because besides you, I'll have to contend with the entire cast and chorus of the Opera Company of Seville, not to mention Her Royal Highness, Señorita Estela Moreno."

"Who's she, pray tell?"

"Oh, you'll meet dear Estela soon enough, although you might regret it when you do. She's our very talented and beautiful prima donna." Anita sniffed disapprovingly before turning to the mirror above her vanity. She stopped long enough to apply the finishing touches to her elaborate makeup.

"I take it you don't care for Miss Moreno?" Dallas's mind flashed back to Rick's comment about plump prima donnas, but she had a sneaking suspicion that this particular one didn't have a weight problem.

"Let's just say she isn't one of my favorite people," Anita rejoined dryly. She pursed her sensuous lips to color them with bright coral from a tube of Lancôme. Dallas crossed to the bed and perched there, in no real hurry to get downstairs. Because of the language barrier, she hadn't been all that keen about attending the reception in the first place, but she had given her word to Rick that she would be there.

"Unfortunately, the men around here feel quite differently about Estela," Anita went on. "She and Rick have been friendly for years. As a matter of fact, she was one of his biggest supporters when the members of the symphony association were voting on which architect to use for the new theater." Anita leaned away from the mirror, inspected her face critically, then fluffed her pseudo-windswept mass of curls, arranging a few on her smooth forehead. Her hair had an auburn sheen beneath the bedroom's ceiling lights.

"Really, I don't understand what they see in her, apart from her looks, of course. I can't deny that she's attractive in the classic Spanish style . . . you know, the jet black hair and dark almond-shaped eyes and that flawless ivory skin."

"She's not married, then?" Dallas's throat was curiously tight as she pictured Rick attached to a woman of that caliber.

"No, as far as I know she's always been single. Supposedly she's totally dedicated to her art—and she is very, very good. But I just bet she'd sacrifice her career in a New York minute if the right man demanded it." Anita gazed speculatively at Dallas, adding, "Wouldn't we all?"

The hotel's largest ballroom, opulently decorated in gold, alabaster and garnet red and lighted by two enormous crystal chandeliers, was packed to overflowing when Dallas and Anita made their entrance minutes later. Apparently, nearly every member of the cast, crew and orchestra had decided to attend, their number nearly doubled by the fact that most were accompanied by spouses or escorts of one description or another.

Dallas's fear of being overdressed was instantly dispelled when she viewed the others in attendance. No doubt some would consider her apparel modest compared to the flamboyant outfits sported by a number of guests. She wondered with amusement if some of them realized they were not on stage at the moment.

As she followed Anita, brushing past countless shoulders, her gaze wandered over the boisterous European crowd. She sighted Rick easily, for he towered over nearly everyone in the ballroom. Dark-jacketed and smiling, he stood deep in conversation with a stunning voluptuous woman attired in a close-fitting dress of crimson lace. Her lustrous sable-dark hair was severely combed back from her regal face and knotted in a glamorous chignon at the back of her head.

Anita had spotted her brother as well. She grabbed Dallas's arm and dragged her across the marble floor until they reached him and his striking companion.

"Rick . . . Estela, *qué tal?*" Anita chimed.

"Ah, *hermanita*," Rick drawled, greeting his sister. Then his attention turned to Dallas. Her pulse skipped erratically as his narrowed gaze traveled slowly and approvingly over her dress. Belatedly, his eyes met hers. "*Hola*, Dallas," he said, flashing an indolent smile. "I'm glad you could make it."

Next, he turned to the woman at his side. "Estela, may I present Señorita Dallas Jones from America."

"How nice to meet you," the older woman said, her faintly-accented voice silvery and melodious, yet coolly reserved. "I understand that you, too, are a student of music." Estela Moreno's thick-lashed ebony eyes shrewdly appraised Dallas. "You are a coloratura perhaps?"

"A lyric soprano," Dallas replied politely. This seemed to momentarily relieve Estela's competitive nature, and she smilingly drew her young rival into a discussion about the future of opera in the United States, where she said she'd performed several times.

Soon they were joined by an attractive Spaniard, fortyish, with wiry brown hair above a deeply-grooved forehead. He stood several inches shorter than Rick. The man's dark appreciative gaze roved over each of the three women in turn, finally coming to rest on the fairest one.

"I do not believe I have had the pleasure, *señorita*," purred the rich, strongly-accented baritone voice.

"You don't waste any time, eh, Miguel?" Estela flicked a disdainful glance his way. The newcomer merely grinned, delighted to have ruffled the beautiful prima donna's feathers.

Rick scowled, no more pleased than Estela with the man's arrival. Anita alone remained unperturbed, even beaming a welcome. "Please meet Miss Dallas Jones of Texas, Miguel," she invited. "Dallas, this is Miguel Rivera—"

"You must call me Miguel, *señorita*," he said, taking Dallas's hand and carrying it to his lips. Ironically, she felt far less threatened by this overt Latin charmer than she did by Rick, who at this point was frowning broadly. Amusement played over her face as Miguel kissed her hand, holding it much longer than necessary.

"Miguel is our company's esteemed director," Estela explained, a note of sarcasm flattening her melodic voice.

Dallas found this information not at all surprising. The man had a suave, yet dynamic presence and the alert, intelligent eyes of a maestro.

"Dallas is a singer, too, Miguel," Anita chimed in.

"*Verdad?* Is that so?" the conductor exclaimed, his mouth widening into a captivating smile. "We must get better acquainted then. Come, *señorita* . . . have a drink with me."

Before Dallas could respond, she was being whisked across the ballroom away from the others.

She cast a single glance behind her fluttering skirt, wincing at the lingering look of displeasure carved on Rick's darkly handsome face. She had only a moment to ponder his apparent dislike for Miguel Rivera before the charming Spaniard was pressing a glass into her hand and smiling into her wide blue eyes.

"Tell me, *señorita*, how do you happen to be in *Sevilla*?"

"Please call me Dallas."

"I am most honored to do so," he said smoothly.

She briefly recounted the auto accident, Eula's condition, and the assistance rendered by the Santanas.

Miguel Rivera shrugged expressively. "It appears that you may find it necessary to remain in our beautiful city indefinitely."

"At this point I'm really not sure how much longer we'll be staying," Dallas admitted. "There were some minor complications, and thankfully Dr. Hidalgo is taking no chances with my aunt's health."

"Yes, I know Roberto. He is an excellent physician." Miguel paused, before going on. "Let us hope that you and your aunt will be here at least until the opening of our production of *Don Giovanni*."

Dallas's face brightened. "So that's the opera you'll be doing. How exciting for you. It's one of my all-time favorites."

"Mine as well," Miguel said. "I am most happy with our rehearsals of late . . . with only one exception." His narrow face crinkled into a mild frown.

"Oh, what's that?"

"One of my performers—Andrea Santa María, a

wonderful young soprano—is having terrible problems with her throat." His hand moved to his neck in an illustrative massage. "She has—how do you say?—*nodes*? on her vocal cords. I am concerned because the role of Zerlina, although not the principal female part, is a significant one."

"Yes, indeed," Dallas agreed sympathetically. "What a pity for your soprano. Zerlina is such a delight to sing."

Miguel's face went from astonished to hopeful. "You know Zerlina?" he demanded. "You are familiar with this role?"

"Why, yes," she replied. "As a matter of fact, I performed it this past spring at the Santa Fe Opera in New Mexico. It was great fun. Our director was very pleased with—" Dallas broke off in surprise when Miguel's urgent question interrupted her.

"Tell me, *señorita* . . . did they use the original Italian libretto?"

"Uh-huh." Dallas smiled reminiscently. "You know, I really prefer the Italian to any of the English translations."

"*Madre de Dios!*" Miguel's voice was jubilant. "I cannot believe what I am hearing!" An exultant expression transformed his face. "The saints are truly smiling down on Miguel Rivera this day." He caught both of Dallas's hands in his. "My dear Señorita Jones . . . you are the answer to a prayer."

"Hey, now wait a minute," Dallas protested, finally aware of the direction his thoughts had taken.

"Please—please, tell me you will do it." Miguel

proceeded as if she hadn't said a word. "You must be my new Zerlina!" His voice rose with excitement, and he lifted his hand to finger a golden lock of hair curled at her shoulder. "It will be a shame to cover this with a black wig, but I think we must, eh?"

"Whoa . . . slow down a minute," Dallas quickly cut in. "Look *Señor*—Miguel—be realistic, won't you? You've never heard me sing. How do you even know that you'd like my voice?" She sighed in exasperation as he launched into another stream of animated chatter.

"Dallas, *querida*, you will be perfect! I feel this in my soul. Trust me, *por favor.*"

"But Miguel, your staging and choreography will be totally different." Overcome with indecision, but more than a trifle intrigued, Dallas gnawed her bottom lip.

"A mere technicality, *bellissima.* We have exactly one week in which to overcome such problems," he said confidently. "Say that you will come to my rehearsal tomorrow."

She sighed heavily. "I don't know—" A week wasn't a lot of time, especially when she would be working in a foreign environment. His idea was outrageous, yet. . . .

"Come, Dallas, admit that what I propose is an irresistible, exciting challenge!"

"A challenge definitely." Dallas paused, grimacing. "I'm not too sure about the irresistible part," she said, raising confused eyes heavenward. "Seriously, Miguel, what about—what's her name?—Andrea? Is there any chance her throat will be healed enough for her to be able to perform for the premiere?"

"A very small one, perhaps, but I do not have much hope of it."

"Isn't there anyone else—someone in the chorus maybe—who can handle the role? Didn't she have an understudy?"

"Of course, but I am not satisfied with Teresa. She cannot act, poor girl, and her voice is a little weak. She herself knows this and fears the part. As for the others in the chorus, no one is—how can I explain?— star quality!" He glowed with pride when he located the English words he was searching for.

Dallas again tossed her head in exasperation. "Miguel! What gives you the idea that I'm star quality?" she demanded, hands on her hips.

He chuckled sensuously. "I have already told you, *querida.*" His deep voice caressed her. "I feel this in my soul . . . and I am known to be clairvoyant about such things." He shrugged and gestured with his hands. "You have the look," he stated emphatically.

How could she help but return that infectious smile? The man was the most potent charmer she'd ever met. Her brain was reeling with possibilities and excitement. When she still hesitated to give him an affirmative answer, Miguel spoke again.

"Please at least attend our rehearsal at eleven o'clock in the morning, Dallas," he urged. "You have nothing to lose, *verdad*? With your aunt in the hospital, you have time on your hands, eh? When we have finished, you will be free to return to America with a performance in Spain to add to your list of musical accomplishments."

This was precisely what had been running through her mind during their conversation. A European performance on her résumé would be quite an achievement in her young career. Dr. Klimash would be beside himself to learn that she had done *Don Giovanni* abroad. It was much too good to be true!

"What can I say, Miguel? You're absolutely right." Dallas grinned resignedly. Her heart skipped in excited anticipation.

The next moment she found both of her hands grabbed and subjected to numerous kisses from the enthused lips of Maestro Miguel Rivera.

Chapter Six

Miguel spent the next hour propelling Dallas around the reception, happily introducing her to various cast members, most of whom greeted the pretty foreigner with reserved warmth. It didn't take her long to realize that she would have to prove herself before they would really accept her into their fellowship. And she would, she vowed, feeling a surge of confidence and eagerness. Miguel's jubilant mood was contagious, spurring her to rise to the challenge of this fabulous and unexpected opportunity.

In the midst of her introduction to Felipe Quiroga, the stocky young baritone who was to play Zerlina's fiancé, Masetto, Dallas heard a familiar female voice call her name.

"Here you are," Anita said with a laugh. "I was

89

beginning to wonder if Miguel had permanently abducted you."

"Not quite yet, Anita *mía*, but I am in the process of doing so." Miguel bowed to them, begging to be excused to go in search of Estela. "I must tell her the fantastic news! Come, Felipe."

"What news is he talking about?" Anita demanded, watching the two men fade into the crowd.

"You won't believe it when I tell you. In fact, I'm still not sure that I do." Dallas sighed, launching into a hasty explanation.

"That *is* great news!" Anita declared. "I bet you'll be marvelous. Just don't let Estela give you a hard time."

"Would she do that?" Dallas's delicate brow crinkled.

"Estela doesn't like sharing the limelight with anyone," Anita explained, "particularly someone who looks like you. Didn't you notice the way she scoped you out?"

"She did seem a little cool." Dallas shook her head dismissively. "Look, I shouldn't pose a threat to someone in her league," Dallas insisted. "She's an experienced professional. I'm a novice in comparison."

"She may not see it that way," Anita warned.

"Well, never fear, dahlin'." Dallas fluttered her lashes while performing her best Texas drawl. "We southern belles can plum sure take care of ourselves."

Anita giggled. "I believe it! Now, where did Tony disappear to?" She glanced around, scanning the crowd.

"How is that going?" Dallas wanted to know.

"Well, I really thought we were making progress." Anita smiled reminiscently. "We danced in the Oasis and it was heavenly."

"So I noticed."

Anita caught Dallas's teasing look and smiled crookedly. "It was that obvious, huh?"

"Afraid so." She reached out to touch the brunette's arm. "Seriously, Anita, if you want to keep your brother in the dark, I would watch my step if I were you. He isn't exactly blind."

"An accurate observation, *chica*," a deep male voice spoke at her back.

Dallas and Anita whirled around simultaneously. The latter looked positively stricken as her brother moved to stand beside them. There was no way to know how much of their conversation he'd overheard.

"So tell me, *hermana* . . . what am I being kept in the dark about?" His black brows lifted inquiringly.

"Er, well . . . uh, it's a surprise actually . . . isn't that right, Dallas?" Anita glanced frantically at her friend for support. "You see, Miguel and Dallas have a little surprise, and it—" Her voice trailed off lamely when she noted the scowl materializing on her brother's face.

"I don't much care for surprises," he said. His smooth-shaven jaw seemed to tighten.

Dallas's anxious glance darted from one to the other, unsure of the next move. Deciding a forceful attack was the only hope, she charged ahead, regretting her words even as she uttered them. "It's really none of your business, Rick."

"I don't know what kind of game this is, *niñas*, but I'm not in the mood." His narrowed eyes assumed the disturbing color of Texas storm clouds, making Dallas fervently wish that she was home in Austin at that very moment.

"It's nothing to be concerned about, Rick, honestly," Anita hastened, patting his arm in a placating gesture. But her brother would not be deterred.

"If you're planning to get involved with Rivera in any way whatsoever, you're playing with fire," he told Dallas in a terse voice.

"Thanks for the advice," she retorted, "but I think I'm adult enough to choose my own friends."

"I beginning to wonder about that," Rick remarked.

Dallas was stung by his tone.

"Hey, wait, you two . . . please!" Anita interrupted pleadingly. "This is all my fault. Rick, let me explain—"

"No!" cried Dallas, finding her voice again. It was obvious that Anita was prepared to confess her feelings for Antonio, and that might prove disastrous. "This is between me and your brother," Dallas told her sharply.

Anita's mouth formed a protest which Dallas waved aside, murmuring, "Let me handle this, okay?" Their gazes locked momentarily, exchanging silent messages, then Anita nodded. Looking grim, she moved away in search of her boss.

"I'm waiting," Rick said gruffly.

Dallas's mind groped feverishly for words. Since she was forced to make use of the cover story impulsively supplied by Anita, Dallas rushed on saying: "You're overreacting, Rick. Miguel invited me to sing with the opera company, that's all."

"Why would you want to keep that from me?" he demanded.

"Your sister thought it would be fun to surprise you," Dallas lied, crossing her fingers behind her back. "Obviously, Anita was wrong."

Rick was quiet for a moment, presumably trying to absorb Dallas's explanation. She watched him with anxious eyes, wishing she could read his mind to assure herself that he'd been satisfied with her story.

"I don't like it," he said at last.

"What?" Confusion marred Dallas's face.

"Rivera is bad news. It would be a mistake for you to get involved with him."

"Let's get one thing straight, Rick Santana," Dallas said heatedly. "The fact that I'm staying in your hotel doesn't give you the right to interfere in my personal business. I've already committed to sing for Miguel."

"So tell him you've changed your mind," Rick suggested impatiently.

"No," Dallas retorted, appalled at his attitude.

"Rivera is a notorious womanizer," Rick said in a low tone. "You don't have the experience to handle a man like that."

"Miguel is interested in my *voice*," Dallas insisted icily, "and contrary to your arbitrary assessment, I *can* handle him." Her fists punched into her hips for emphasis. "I'm not a child, you know."

She gasped indignantly when a mirthless laugh broke from Rick's lips. "No, you're just acting like one," he commented, "a very spoiled one, who seems used to getting her own way."

Speechless with fury, Dallas twirled from him with finesse worthy of Seville's finest flamenco dancers. She charged through the ballroom to the exit, hot tears of anger and resentment scalding her eyes. *How dare he say such things! What makes him think he has the right to tell me not to become involved with Miguel?* She wouldn't even have met the conductor in the first place if Rick hadn't insisted that she attend the blasted reception. Just because she'd been forced to endure Rick's hospitality didn't give him an open license to try and run her life. There was just no getting around it—the man could be an absolute tyrant! Somehow she would have to escape from the Palacio Moro . . . as soon as possible.

Dallas dried her burning eyes and was reaching for the zipper of her dress when a loud staccato knock assaulted the door, startling her. The force of the pounding told her it had to be Rick. She approached the door cautiously, her heart rioting in her chest.

"Go away . . . leave me alone!" she called out.

"Open the door, Dallas," growled the familiar voice, confirming her suspicions.

For long moments she stood speechless, chewing her lips, her mind desperately searching for a reply.

Realizing suddenly that Rick might use his passkey, she whipped the deadbolt in place with a crack. A wave of apprehension washed over her when the tenacious hammering commenced again.

"I have nothing left to say to you, Mr. Santana, so please just go away," she cried.

Several more tense moments elapsed before Rick announced threateningly: "I'll stand out here all night if necessary."

All at once their shouting match seemed comical to Dallas. The strain of the last few hours had taken its toll on her nerves. She began to laugh uncontrollably, releasing some of the pent-up tension in her body. Finally, after recovering her composure, she stepped forward, slid the deadbolt back with quivering fingers, and opened the door to admit a fuming Rick. The annoyed look darkening his face suggested he had not been similarly affected by the humor of the situation.

Instantly sober, Dallas shut the door and leaned against it. Her uneasy mind was already questioning the wisdom of letting him inside.

"You really try my patience, *mujer*," Rick grated. He towered over her, grinding his expensive shoes into the carpet like a bull getting ready for the charge.

Feeling abruptly weary, Dallas gazed up at him. "Please, Rick . . . I don't want to argue with you anymore tonight. I'm really exhausted." She raised a hand to her forehead and brushed at her hair in a tired gesture. "Besides, I don't think we have anything else to discuss . . ."

"That's where you're wrong," he rejoined in a determined voice. Wide-eyed, she sucked in her breath when his fingers caught her shoulders to unpeel her from the door. Then he took her hand and led her across the room. "Sit down, hmm?" he said, nudging her into one of the armchairs. He lowered himself into the other one, his hand loosening the tie at his throat.

Dallas felt the impact of his narrowed, unblinking gaze as he studied her pale face across the small table between their chairs. Her pulse quickened, and every fiber in her body tensed. Even with his black hair disheveled and the remnants of wrath in his tanned face, he was incredibly handsome, with those bold, aristocratic features she had noticed the first day they'd met.

"You can relax," Rick began, keeping his gaze fixed on her as he spoke. "Anita confided the entire situation concerning Antonio. She feels rotten that your attempts to conceal her little secret caused an argument between us."

Dallas heaved a sigh of relief. "What exactly did she say—about Tony, I mean?"

"That she has been in love with him for some time, and was afraid to tell me for fear that I would get involved to the detriment of their relationship." Rick's lips quirked. "I'm afraid my dear little sister has been upsetting herself unnecessarily."

"Oh?"

"I've known about her feelings almost from the beginning," he went on. "Anita is remarkably transparent. And I'll tell you something else: although he may not realize it yet, Antonio cares for her as well."

"Really? Oh, Rick, that's wonderful," Dallas exclaimed.

He shrugged. "We'll see."

"If you knew all this, why didn't you do anything to help them out?" Dallas asked, frowning.

"I believed then, as I do now, that they have to work things out for themselves."

"Do you think Anita's right about why Tony is reluctant to get involved with her?"

"We only spoke briefly, but I gather she believes it has something to do with me," Rick responded dryly.

"She said Tony probably feels that getting involved with her would be in violation of your friendship, but to me that's ridiculous," Dallas declared.

Rick gave a short laugh. "I'm not surprised *you* feel that way. I'd hardly expect you to think like a man. And you have no knowledge or awareness of the Spanish sense of honor and propriety," he said, rekindling Dallas's resentment.

"Maybe not," she said, leaning forward and gripping the arms of her chair. "But I do know one thing: you could help Anita if you really wanted to."

"Oh? And what do you suggest, Little Miss Matchmaker?" His tone softened to tease her.

"There must be *something* you can do," Dallas returned defensively. She paused in thought. "Couldn't you tell Tony it would be okay with you if they went out or something?"

"Wouldn't that be a little presumptuous?" Rick snorted. "What would I say? 'Hey, Tony, *mi amigo*

. . . I just want you to know you have my permission to date my sister'?"

"You're impossible!" Dallas flounced back in her chair in vexation.

Rick frowned. "Look, Antonio and Anita are mature, consenting adults. They'll just have to solve their own problems. I'm staying out of it, and so should you. If for some reason they fail to work things out, it just wasn't meant to be."

"Oh, give me a break, Rick," Dallas snapped. "You know darn good and well they'd be happy together, yet you won't lift a finger to help them."

Rick leaned forward. His stormy eyes flashed a warning. "This conversation is beginning to grow tedious, Dallas."

"Then why don't you leave?" she suggested tartly, rising and crossing to the door. Her hand rested on the knob and she shot him a frigid look over her shoulder.

He stood slowly, his expression unreadable, before four long strides brought him an arm's length away from her.

"I'm not quite finished with what I came in here to say," he informed her quietly.

"Well, what is it?" She rolled her eyes.

"I'm serious about Rivera. I don't think you should get involved with him."

"Oh, please! Not again," Dallas choked in frustration. "I *told* you . . . the man is interested in me as a musician, nothing more."

Rick's brows furrowed thoughtfully as he appeared to evaluate this idea. "So, you think if he tries anything, you can handle him?" he questioned her consideringly.

Dallas was secretly amazed that Rick had assumed the role of protective big brother, especially after their earlier encounters when he'd acted anything but brotherly. "Of course I can handle him," she insisted in an aggravated tone.

Rick's piercing gaze caught hers and held it with such magnetic force she was incapable of looking away. "Prove it," he challenged softly.

"What?" Her eyes were wary. When his meaning registered, her heart bounded. "I think you'd better go," she said.

"I'm not leaving until you show me you can cope with a red-blooded Latin male." With that, Rick reached for her, dragging her into his powerful arms.

Furiously determined to put him in his place, Dallas wedged her arms between his chest and hers. "Let go of me . . . I mean it, Rick!" she cried, her voice sharp with ire.

His eyes were brimming with mischief. "What if I don't want to?" he mocked lightly.

"Don't *make* me hurt you," she threatened, quite serious.

Laughter spilled from his grinning mouth, infuriating her further. His grip on her relaxed as he started to say something. Seizing the opportunity, she shoved at his shoulders, creating enough room between them to enable her to kick him soundly in the shin.

"Ow! *Bruja*—witch!" Rick grunted in surprise. "That was a low blow," he complained, but amusement crept back into his smoldering eyes. His long fingers curled around her upper arms, imprisoning her still.

"I warned you," Dallas retorted loftily. "Don't force me to do it again."

"Okay, you've made your point," he grudgingly conceded. "You can handle yourself in a pinch. I'm impressed."

"Now let me go," she commanded, even though that was the last thing in the world she really wanted. In truth, she would have preferred to remain in his arms indefinitely, like during their dance in the Oasis.

"Before I leave," Rick said softly, "I believe you owe me a kiss." He drew her closer until she was against him, her hands flattened on his chest.

"For what?" Her suspicious gaze locked with his, but her heart began to throb with excitement.

"To make up for kicking me, *mujer*."

Quivering in anticipation, Dallas didn't protest when his hand lifted to her head. "You deserved it," she charged breathlessly.

"And you deserve this . . ." His fingers were deftly tangled in a mass of golden curls. With a small tug, he urged her head back. Then his mouth was gently covering hers.

His hands shifted around her as he tenderly made her his willing captive against the wall beside the door. Then his lips trailed lightly across her face to the perfumed hollow below her ear. "You maddening little witch," he whispered, his warm breath tingling her sensitive skin. "I can't be in the same room as you without wanting to hold you . . . and kiss you."

"I—I'm not sure this is a good idea. . . ." There was a thread of desperation in her faint voice. Never before with any other man had she felt so in danger of losing control over her emotions. It rendered her totally vulnerable in the secluded lamplit setting of her hotel room.

"It's the best idea I've had in years," came Rick's husky rejoinder. He bent his head again. His mouth began a slow, gentle path across her forehead and down her cheek, hesitating at the edge of her parted lips.

"I'll be gone for a few days—I have some business to take care of in Madrid," he said in a low voice, pausing to gain control of his heightened breathing. "Remember what I said about Miguel Rivera."

With that, Rick whipped open the door. He vanished into the hallway before Dallas was capable of offering a protest to his unsolicited advice.

Chapter Seven

Dallas's first rehearsal with the Opera Company of Seville was child's play compared to her encounters with Rick Santana. Miguel Rivera oozed Spanish charm as he formally introduced her to the cast and crew, many of whom she'd already met at the previous night's reception.

Her test of fire came almost at once, when Miguel suggested that she entertain the group by performing the famous seduction scene duet, *"Là ci darem la mano,"* with the rakish Don Giovanni, played by Sergio Sopranzi, a middle-aged Italian invited to star in the special summer production.

With proverbial butterflies fluttering wildly in her stomach, Dallas joined a grinning, enthusiastic Sergio on the wide stage. With scores in hand, they launched into the delightful duet. Dallas had no difficulty blending artistically with Sergio's smooth, vibrant baritone. Her lyrical voice soared easily across the beautiful new theater, for whose excellent acoustics she silently complimented the architect. By the time she and Sergio reached the final notes of the song, their audience was standing, cheering and applauding hearty approval. Dallas smiled and curtsied prettily, bowing to a triumphant Sergio, who took her hand and graciously carried it to his mustachioed lips.

"Brava! Fantastico!" Miguel was elated. "Did I not say she would be perfect, Sergio? Felipe? Dallas, *querida*, you sing like an angel! Come, everyone, let us begin the rehearsal."

The only individual who appeared rather unimpressed with the performance was the beautiful Estela Moreno. She sighed as though bored throughout the duet, and although she applauded perfunctorily during the ovation, she didn't seem to share the sentiments of her fellow cast members.

Teresa, the young understudy for the part of Zerlina, proved to be a wonderfully good sport. She approached Dallas immediately with sincere congratulations. "I'm so happy Miguel found you, *señorita*. I'm just not ready for such an important role. It frightens me."

Dallas smiled sympathetically at the pretty redhead, insisting that Teresa call her by her first name. "Have you been in the chorus long?" she asked the girl.

"Almost three years," Teresa replied in her sweet

accented voice. "The money is not very good, but we're a big happy family."

"That means a lot, I know."

After several hours of intense rehearsals, Dallas found her throat a bit sore and made a mental note to ask Anita if she could use one of the pianos in the hotel to do daily warm-up scales and exercises. She felt the neglect in her voice from not having sung in several weeks.

Miguel, still in high spirits from his recent discovery, announced a two-hour break. "Come lunch with us, Dallas," he invited.

She hesitated only a moment, recalling Rick's warning, then promptly dismissed it from her mind. It was foolish to try and deny her attraction to him, but she wasn't about to allow him to dictate her behavior.

As much as she wanted to see him, she was almost grateful that he was away on business. With the thrilling challenge of *Don Giovanni* before her, the last thing she needed to distract her from doing her best was Rick Santana. Her pulse reacted every time she recalled her helpless response to his kisses.

That morning over breakfast Dallas had rededicated herself to her decision to seek accommodations elsewhere at the earliest opportunity. Soon Eula would be released from the hospital, and together they could afford a nice hotel room well below the Palacio Moro's steep rates. Besides, it made good sense to move closer to the opera house, as well as to the hospital, since Eula would be under Roberto's care for several more weeks.

* * *

The restaurant was located on Plaza Vírgen de los Reyes, near the gigantic gothic Cathedral of Seville, one of the largest churches in the world. Its famous tower, known as La Giralda, was originally the minaret of an Almohad mosque, Miguel told Dallas.

"You must visit the interior," he recommended. "There are many treasures, including a number of Murillo's paintings and works by Zurbarán, Morales and Goya."

The conductor had included Estela, Sergio and Felipe in his luncheon invitation. A waiter escorted the group of five to a table in the center of the crowded restaurant. Dallas noticed interested glances being cast their way, and concluded that the other members of her party were probably well-known celebrities in the city.

Over plates of roasted chicken and potatoes, they chatted amiably throughout their leisurely lunch break. Out of courtesy to Dallas and Sergio, the Spaniards spoke primarily in English.

"*Maestro*, was there really a Don Giovanni—a Don Juan? Did he actually exist?" asked Felipe Quiroga during a lull in the conversation.

"An excellent question, *mi amigo*," Miguel replied.

"I thought he was a fictional character in a Spanish play," Dallas interposed, as interested as young Felipe to learn more.

"Ah, yes, *El Burlador de Sevilla* by Tirso de Molina." Miguel nodded thoughtfully. "Some historians claim that the tale of Don Juan's adventures was well known in Spain long before it was dramatized by

Tirso. Who really knows for certain if Don Juan was a legendary figure or a flesh-and-blood man?" A roguish grin separated Miguel's lips. "I suspect there have been countless Don Juans throughout the centuries, and there will continue to be . . . men who dedicate their life to the amorous pursuit of feminine beauty."

"You should know," Estela broke in acidly. The three men at the table chortled in unison.

"Personally, I can't imagine why any woman would be interested in that type of man," Dallas commented. Estela cast a rather frosty glance at her while the men's noisy humor faded.

"Dallas, *querida*, you are so young, so very innocent," Miguel said, a paternal note in his voice. "For some women, a man such as Don Juan represents all that is attractive, as well as dangerous, in a male. They are fascinated by him and intrigued by the challenge to tame him."

"That may be," she allowed with a sigh. "Still, I could never be drawn to a man like that."

Miguel smiled at her. "The one who is fortunate enough to win your love will no doubt be more than satisfied having you alone. He won't want or need to seek diversion with other women."

"That's very sweet of you, Miguel," Dallas murmured, a little embarrassed. Then she found herself wondering if Rick would ever settle down with one woman. It disturbed her profoundly whenever she started to imagine how many women before her had experienced his kisses.

Moments later Estela appeared to read Dallas's mind. "Speaking of exceptional men, I talked to Ricardo Santana this morning." The shapely diva fairly purred with female appreciation.

Dallas's heart jolted in dismay, but she maintained a casual expression. Miguel's face, on the other hand, visibly hardened.

"Ricardo called me before departing for Madrid," Estela went on conversationally, "to assure me that his staff will make every effort to locate my bracelet."

"Your bracelet?" Felipe frowned.

"Yes, my canary diamond bracelet has simply disappeared," Estela explained with theatrical verve. "I am quite distraught over it. The bracelet was a gift I received while performing *Lucia di Lammermoor* in Sydney two years ago. It must have slipped off my arm at the Palacio Moro."

"You wore it to the party?" Dallas surmised.

"Of course not," the brunette responded condescendingly. "I had my rubies on last evening. They match the dress I was wearing perfectly." Apparently, she was affronted that Dallas hadn't noticed her jewels at the reception. "I remember having my canary bracelet on last week when I was lunching with Ricardo at the hotel." Estela's shoulders effected a dramatic shrug. "And now, I cannot locate it anywhere."

"What will you do if they are unable to find it?" Sergio wanted to know.

"I will be most desolate," the soprano declared, adopting a pouty look. "It was, after all, one of my finest pieces." Then her dark eyes gleamed with speculation. "However, I'm sure if Ricardo cannot locate it at the hotel, he will arrange to compensate me quite generously . . . in one way or another," she cooed with a coquettish smile.

A sharp pain lodged in the pit of Dallas's stomach as she visualized Rick with this sophisticated woman. Suddenly, she lost her appetite for dessert.

Unusually quiet, Miguel motioned for the check, and minutes later they were headed back to the theater.

The week of rehearsals passed swiftly, a blur of long hours and grueling work, but one of the best times Dallas had ever had. She was taxed to the limits of her physical and mental capabilities, savoring every minute of this priceless learning experience. Her sincere, conscientious attitude made her an instant favorite with many of the cast and crew, all dedicated professionals whose common goal was the ultimate success of the production.

Arguments were rare, and the few times they materialized tended to involve Miguel and his temperamental leading lady. Estela seemed determined to have the last word on any scene in which her character, Donna Anna, figured prominently. Wisely, Dallas kept out of her way as much as possible.

The day Eula was released from the hospital, Dallas procured an attractive, comfortable room at the Hotel Argentina, a moderately-priced establishment located a few blocks from the opera house. Anita had been reticent about helping her to find alternate accommodations, but finally gave in when it became clear that Dallas was serious about leaving the Palacio Moro.

"At least have some of your meals here," Anita had pleaded.

"I don't know," Dallas equivocated. "I'll be really tied up with rehearsals for the next few days." She finally agreed to let Anita send a car for her and Eula that night around eight. Roberto Hidalgo was invited and joined them in the Torre del Oro Restaurant as arranged.

It was an enjoyable evening of good food and pleasant conversation. After dessert, as Roberto and Eula relaxed, heads bent together, engrossed in their own dialogue, Dallas leaned toward Anita.

"So tell me," she prompted, "how is the romance going?"

Anita laughed softly, her green eyes aglow. "I've been itching for an opportunity to talk to you," she admitted. "We're making definite progress now."

"Really?" Dallas chimed. "What's been going on?"

"Well, you know Rick has been out of town—"

Dallas nodded, the mention of his name an instant stimulant to her emotions.

"So I've been much less inhibited around Tony, and he around me," Anita said. "I think Rick makes him a little nervous—where I'm concerned, that is."

"I can appreciate that," Dallas murmured. "Go on."

"The big news is . . . Tony actually kissed me!" Anita looked radiant.

Dallas forced a smile as she found herself wistfully recalling a different kiss entirely.

"It was so wonderful, Dallas! Just as I had always imagined it would be. We were working on the accounts late yesterday . . . alone in my office. It all seemed to happen in slow motion. I was in my chair, and he was standing beside me bending over the books. I looked up at him with a question about the laundry expenses, our eyes met, and suddenly he was kissing me like he couldn't help himself." She beamed reminiscently. "Poor darling was so embarrassed when he finally stopped. You notice I said 'he stopped,' because I can tell you I had no intention of stopping!"

Anita's excitement was contagious. "What did he do then?" Dallas asked, truly delighted for her friend.

"Oh, he mumbled something about checking on the night crew and took off without another word."

"So how is he behaving today?"

"Ha! He's been avoiding me like the devil, but I refuse to be depressed about it. I'm positive that he loves me. All I have to do now is get him to admit it to himself . . . and to my brother." Anita paused, a serene and happy calm transforming her features.

"I've got it!" Dallas exclaimed. "Why don't you invite Antonio to the opera on Saturday night? *Don Giovanni* might be just the thing to inspire him into chasing you." She flashed a self-satisfied smile at the brilliance of her idea.

"Great idea!" Anita cried. "But what if Tony refuses to go?"

"Tell him I insisted you both attend, because I expect everybody I know to be there to witness my European début," Dallas ended with a mockingly regal air.

Anita giggled. "I sure hope Rick gets back in time for opening night," she said after a pause. "I know he would really like to hear you sing, too."

Dallas's throat constricted painfully. It had never occurred to her that Rick might work one of her performances into his busy schedule. Why did the thought of his critical appraisal unnerve her when she had been singing, as well as acting, before countless audiences for most of her life? She was reminded of her freshman year at the University of Texas School of Music. She'd quickly developed a crush on a senior student named Stephen Hamilton, the lead tenor in her first opera workshop. Near the end of the semester, Dallas was asked to sing a solo. To her acute dismay, she came close to freezing on stage when Stephen happened to stroll into the theater during the opening notes of the aria. Over the years that followed, she had learned to conquer such episodes one of her professors called "performance anxiety." Now, Dallas cringed inwardly. Why did the mere mention of Rick's name cause that debilitating emotional response that she hadn't felt in years?

"Have you heard from your brother?" she asked Anita, keeping her tone casual.

"He calls every day to keep tabs on things, and he's supposed to be back by the weekend." Anita sighed. "I haven't told him that you've moved out, or that you're working with Miguel. You know, I can't quite figure out why Rick is so down on him lately. I've always liked Miguel, and I think his reputation of being a womanizer is grossly exaggerated." She grinned. "Sometimes I think he acts that way just to get a rise out of precious Estela." Anita's attention abruptly shifted to a point over Dallas's head across the crowded dining room. "Hey look, there's Tony! Shall we inaugurate our little conspiracy now?"

"This is as good a time as any," Dallas responded. "Why don't you let me handle it, okay?"

Anita nearly cackled. "The last time I heard that line you and my brother almost had a fist fight!"

"Er, that's true." Dallas's lips twitched in a guilty curve. "All right . . . you do the inviting. I'll play second string."

Excusing themselves from Eula and Roberto, they crossed the restaurant to join Antonio Baez. He was standing by the kitchen door conversing with one of the chefs.

"*Qué tal*, Anita . . . Dallas?" He nodded, an aloof expression on his face.

"Tony, we were just talking about the opera company. You know, they're performing Mozart's *Don Giovanni* on Saturday night. Dallas will be singing, and I really want to go." She paused expectantly.

"By all means go, Anita. I don't expect you to work on Saturday night," her boss replied, puzzlement in his dark eyes.

"You don't get it, Tony," she blurted.

Realizing her friend was already in trouble, Dallas interceded. "What Anita's trying to say, Tony, is that

I would like for all of you to be there for my big opening night. Dr. Hidalgo is escorting my aunt, and I'd love for you to come, too. Please say you will. I really need all the moral support I can get." She focused her most enticing smile at the young Spaniard.

"*Sí, por supuesto*—of course I will attend the opera, Dallas. I wouldn't think of missing it," he assured her.

"Great," Anita chimed, sighing with relief. "Pick me up at seven, would you, Tony?" Ignoring the surprise on his face, she turned to Dallas. "Let's get back to your aunt before Roberto has her running away with him to the *casbah*." She giggled.

"I don't think Eula will be running anywhere anytime soon," Dallas replied with a grimace.

"That's fine with us. We adore having you around, right, Tony?"

The perplexed manager muttered something indistinguishable, excused himself and hastened away.

"Do you think he suspected a conspiracy, Anita?" Dallas asked thoughtfully.

"Maybe, but who cares? He's going, isn't he?"

Friday morning Dallas awakened early, wishing to do some shopping before the eleven o'clock rehearsal called by Miguel the day before. Since arriving in Seville, she had run out of toothpaste, shampoo and a few other necessities. She headed for a large *farmacia* located about a block from the Hotel Argentina where she knew she could find some favorite American brands.

The mid-morning sun was warm on her back as she

retraced her steps in the direction of the hotel, her shoulder bag swinging freely at her side. She had learned to dress lightly in the hot southern climate and was comfortably clad in a flowered cotton blouse, khaki slacks and flat-heeled navy sandals.

Absorbed in daydreams in which Rick Santana figured prominently, she belatedly sensed a presence at her elbow. With a startled glance sideways, she saw a curly-haired teen whose dirty hand was in the process of snatching her purse. With a strangled sound, Dallas jerked away from him, yanking her bag against her side.

An ugly sneer transformed the thief's face when he realized his victim wasn't as defenseless as he'd originally anticipated. He lunged forward, reached again for the purse and managed to secure the shoulder strap. He gave the strip of leather a vicious tug.

"No you don't, you—!" Dallas cried, refusing to relinquish her hold. In horror she realized that the bag contained not only the supplies she'd just purchased, but her cash, travelers checks, and most importantly, her passport! They struggled, with Dallas becoming increasingly frightened by the young man's persistence and the abrasive Spanish he hurled at her. She didn't understand a word of it, but she suspected his language was as filthy as his hands.

They were only half a block from the hotel's side entrance, but no one was in sight. Dallas screeched as her assailant, growing impatient, shoved her roughly to the pavement, simultaneously ripping the leather strap from her weakened grasp. She groaned in helpless frustration and defeat as she watched him disappear around the corner of the building, her bag held triumphantly in one grimy hand.

Several seconds elapsed. She was still slumped over on the ground, recovering her breath and nursing a badly bruised knee, when she glanced up. Incredulous, she saw the same kid, no longer triumphant, rerounding the corner of the hotel, his collar held securely in Rick's relentless grip. Relief and joy surged through Dallas, robbing her of speech. A tremulous smile lifted the corners of her mouth when Rick dropped the purse in her lap with his free hand.

"Don't move," he ordered. "I'll be back for you as soon as I dispose of this trash." He marched the struggling, scowling boy to the hotel's side entrance and ducked inside to deliver him to security guards.

Still shaken, Dallas slowly rose to her feet, keeping her weight on her left leg to spare the injured one. Rick was back in moments. Pale and wide-eyed, she gaped up at him. His narrowed steely gaze swiftly ran over her, from the top of her shining head to her sandaled feet. Reacting as much to his critical scrutiny as to her recent ordeal, she began to tremble uncontrollably. A soft Spanish oath escaped his lips right before he swept her up into his arms and proceeded to carry her to the hotel entrance. Dizzy with shock, she clung to him, her bag hanging awkwardly over his shoulder. His spicy aftershave acted like a whiff of smelling salts, and Dallas's muddled senses started to clear. She breathed deeply, her face pressed against the column of Rick's tawny throat. There was something indescribably wonderful about being in his arms again. She felt safe and protected. When they reached the Hotel Argentina, a uniformed doorman appeared to admit them. In the small lobby, half a dozen employees hovered about in uncertain expectancy, as if they knew they should be doing something, but weren't quite sure what. Dallas thought she heard one of the hapless group murmur Rick's name in awe.

"As much as I enjoy carrying you around, *niña*, you really must try to be more careful." An exasperated lilt colored Rick's deep voice. He tenderly deposited her on a cushioned divan in one quiet corner of the lobby away from the reception desk. Hands on his hips, he stared down at her. With a shake of his dark head, he gently reprimanded her. "Didn't I tell you that Seville is one of the worst cities in Spain for purse-snatchings? Lucky for you I happened to be in the neighborhood and heard you scream."

"Th-thank you, Rick, really," Dallas stammered. Her heart seemed to turn over in her chest as she gazed at him. He was casually attired in a forest green polo shirt over jeans. She guessed he must have arrived back in town late the night before.

"Let me take a look at your injury," he offered, noticing that she was absently rubbing her leg through her torn slacks.

"No, don't bother—it's nothing," she said. She caught her breath when Rick, in his usual high-handed fashion, ignored her words. He moved to sit facing her on the edge of the couch. Then he carefully eased her pant leg up over her knee, revealing a large patch of bruised, brushburned skin.

"That's a nasty spot," he observed, running lean fingers lightly over her knee in an exploratory manner. Dallas shivered and her teeth clenched. "I'll get the hotel doctor," Rick said, misinterpreting her reaction to his touch. He quickly stood.

"No, Rick, please don't do that," she insisted. "I'm fine, really I am." She covered her knee before easing both legs off of the sofa. Making a gingerly effort to stand, she murmured: "I'll just go up to the room and put some ointment and a bandage on."

He took her arm to steady her. "All right, but I'm going with you, and on the way maybe you can explain what you're doing here."

"How was your trip?" Dallas countered, pretending she hadn't heard him.

"Very productive," he clipped, not diverted in the least. "Now suppose you tell me why you moved out of the Palacio."

Dallas halted her limping progress to the elevators to glare up at him. "Look, Rick . . . you refused to consider my feelings," she declared, "even after I told you I wasn't comfortable staying there without paying my own way. You can't force hospitality on people, you know."

"I just want you close so I can keep an eye on you," he said, his low tone defensive. "I'm concerned about your safety—and evidently with good reason, considering what just happened. Is that so terrible?"

It touched her that he felt a genuine responsibility

to look after her and Eula. "I really appreciate your concern, Rick," she assured him. "And thanks again for the rescue today." She smiled ruefully.

"My pleasure." Then his eyes were searching hers hopefully. "If we agree to accept your credit card, will you come back to the Palacio?" he asked.

"I really like this little hotel, and Aunt Eula has gotten settled in upstairs. Besides, it's closer to the hospital and the opera house—" With a loud gasp, Dallas twisted her wrist to check her watch. The time was ten-forty. "Oh, my heavens! Dress rehearsal starts in twenty minutes. I've got to get to the theater."

His hand dropped from her arm. "So you decided to take Rivera up on his offer?" Rick said stiffly.

"I *told* you I'd made the commitment," she reminded him. "Don't you realize what a wonderful opportunity this is for me?" she hastened in an appealing tone. "I had to take advantage of it. I would have been a fool not to. And everyone involved in the production has been great, especially Miguel—" She winced at Rick's spontaneous frown.

"I was hoping we could spend some time together this weekend," he grumbled, glancing down when an urgent beeping sound interrupted him. He reached for the tiny black box attached to his belt to read the number in the digital display. "It's the Palacio's emergency code," he said. "I have to go."

"I hope it isn't anything serious." Dallas gazed up at him, her expression anxious.

"It's probably that big group from the national karate tournament," he responded dryly. "They've been practicing in the hallways and frightening the tourists."

"When will I see you again?" Dallas blurted, suddenly wishing he didn't have to leave. The fact that she would definitely be late for rehearsal had completely slipped her mind.

Rick looked down at her, his narrowed eyes thoughtful. "I guess that's up to you." With a gruff *"hasta la vista,"* he turned from her and strode swiftly across the small lobby. Feeling wretchedly deflated, Dallas stood staring at his back.

Chapter Eight

An aura of festive excitement and anticipation pervaded the new Opera House of Seville on Saturday night. A long line of eager music *aficionados* wound from half a block down the broad avenue up to the box office, where several flustered clerks were issuing last-minute balcony tickets as fast as currency could change hands.

Backstage, Dallas was being bustled into her colorful peasant costume by a twittering, helpful Teresa.

"Is my wig on straight?" Dallas queried nervously, patting her head with clammy fingers.

"Yes, yes . . . you look beautiful!" Teresa chirped approval.

Dallas gave a shaky laugh. Thanking the smiling girl, she pirouetted before the brightly lighted mirror running the entire length of the dressing room wall. The place was a mess, with clothes strewn everywhere, costume racks in disarray, the long makeup counter dusty with powder and crowded with bottles and containers of every description.

"You mustn't be afraid," Teresa encouraged cheerfully. "The audience will love you as we all do!"

Dallas gave the young understudy an impulsive hug. "You're so good for my ego, *amiga*," she exclaimed. She twirled to take one last look at herself in the mirror, saying, "Come on—we'd better get going."

"Wait," Teresa said. "I need my shawl." Moving to her designated spot on the makeup bar, she reached for the flowered fringed wrap. When she lifted it, a small glittering object slipped from it and bounced with a dull ping on the hardwood floor.

"I'll get it," Dallas offered. She stooped to retrieve the item. It was a brooch—a golden butterfly, its head, body and wings studded with sparkling diamonds, emeralds and rubies.

"This is gorgeous!" Dallas said. "Did Henri give it to you?" she asked, referring to the Spanish girl's boyfriend.

Teresa smiled and nodded, accepting the pin and depositing it in her makeup bag.

Dallas had met Henri Thevenot days before when she and Teresa were snacking at a sidewalk café adjacent to the theater. He was a young, sullen-faced Frenchman, almost rude in his speech, but Teresa had confessed that she'd fallen hopelessly in love with him. She said they planned to marry before the end of the year.

"What does Henri do for a living?" Dallas had inquired when he'd left them, presumably to return to his job.

"He works in one of the tourist shops on Calle Sierpes," had been Teresa's reply.

By the end of the first act of *Don Giovanni*, Dallas, along with Miguel, Estela and the rest of the cast, glowed with every assurance of success. The audience had been wildly receptive to the fine performances inspired by the veteran conductor's expert leadership. Both Dallas's charming duet with Sergio Sopranzi and her flirtatious aria with Felipe Quiroga, were greeted with thunderous applause, giving her added confidence with which to confront the remainder of the opera.

On her way to the dressing room between acts, she ran headlong into surly Henri Thevenot. "Oops! Excuse me, Henri," she exclaimed. Her smile was not returned by the dark Frenchman. "If you're looking for Teresa, she's over there." Dallas pointed over his shoulder.

"*Merci* . . . thank you," he murmured before turning away.

"By the way," Dallas called before he was out of earshot, "that jeweled butterfly you gave Teresa is really beautiful!"

A surprised look, followed by a frown, touched Henri's face before he continued on his way, muttering under his breath.

Briefly wondering how Teresa could possibly be interested in such an unfriendly young man, Dallas hurried to the dressing room, her mind already racing off
in another direction. The performance was going so
well, she found herself wishing that Rick was part of
the audience. Then perhaps he would understand why
it had been so important that she accept this momen-
tous opportunity. But she knew he wasn't out there.
Before she'd departed for the theater earlier in the day,
Anita had phoned to laughingly tell her to "break a
leg."

"Thanks, but Aunt Eula says we have quite enough
bruised and broken bones in the family for one summer," Dallas had returned wryly.

"How true," Anita had chuckled. "Well, then, I'll
just say *buena suerte*—that's 'good luck,' Dallas. And
don't forget, Tony and I will meet you backstage after
the performance."

"Er, what about your brother?" Dallas had managed,
fearful of the answer, but desperate to know. She
hadn't seen nor heard from Rick since their encounter
at the Hotel Argentina on Friday morning. If not for
the opera, which had occupied nearly every minute of
her time, she would have been wallowing in depres-
sion, wondering why he hadn't called.

"I don't believe Rick is going to be able to make
it," Anita had answered apologetically, sensing her
disappointment. "He's heavily involved with a group
of business people working to construct homeless
shelters and clinics in Madrid and Barcelona. It's one

of his favorite projects, and some problems with government permits developed this morning."

Dallas had experienced a pang of guilt at this revelation. She'd never imagined Rick as a philanthropist or a humanitarian; she had only perceived him as a successful capitalist enjoying the "good life." Still, he had been overly generous in his efforts to take care of Eula and her, and she hadn't acted very appreciative in response.

Well, it was for the best that Rick was going to miss the opera, Dallas had finally decided. The mere thought of his critical gaze running over her had the power to send her emotions into turmoil. Wasn't she under enough pressure with this performance? She wanted it to be absolutely perfect—for her fellow musicians and Miguel, for Eula and for her parents, who'd been delighted when she'd phoned home to tell them about her surprise European debut.

The remainder of the opera went as smoothly as the first half, with one amusing exception. During the waning moments, one of the men, zealously overplaying his role, accidentally tread on Estela's flowing gown. The back of her skirt ripped loudly. The other cast members on stage for the finale could hardly contain their merriment at the prima donna's thinly disguised outrage. Professionals to the end, they made it through the last scene without dissolving into hysterical laughter. Seconds later the entire audience was on its feet in riotous applause and cheering. A number of curtain calls followed, more evidence that the production had been an enormous success.

Twenty minutes later Dallas emerged from the dressing room, blond again. She immediately became engulfed in the backstage congratulatory throng. Few people recognized her, and she hastily inched her way through the packed area toward the exit. Her expectant eyes scanned the crowd for some sign of Anita or Antonio.

"Dallas! Over here!" She spun in the direction of Anita's cry, abruptly stopping short, her heart thumping in her chest. Rick stood tall beside his sister. He looked outstanding in dark rich evening wear.

She took a deep breath before brushing through several more sets of shoulders. When she finally reached Anita and Rick, her amethyst voile dress was as ruffled as her taut emotions.

"You were terrific!" Anita squealed, flinging her arms around her friend and hugging her.

"Thank you, *amiga*." Dallas smiled, avoiding Rick's eyes. *Had he been out front in the audience the entire time?* she wondered, her head spinning with the thought. She had been so certain he wasn't coming!

"Bravissima, chica," he said, his tone solemn with admiration. "You were terrific indeed," he added, agreeing with his sister. Dallas gazed up at him, her blue eyes wide with pure happiness, her face flushed with pleasure.

"Let's get you out of here," he murmured, lightly grasping her arm. "The others are waiting in the car. Roberto didn't want your aunt in all this backstage madness."

*   *   *

Jubilation filled the Oasis that night, with few immune to its intoxicating effects. Curious hotel patrons seated near the Santana party's table were witness to the warm camaraderie among the three couples. They saw a handsome older pair, the distinguished gentleman listening attentively to the chattering petite woman; a radiant Spanish beauty gazing adoringly at her dark, attractive companion; and the tall, aristocratic-looking man whose indulgent gaze lingered appreciatively on the blushing young blond at his side.

As Rick and Dallas discussed a variety of topics—including the success of the evening's performance—they discovered they had more in common than just their attraction to each other. He asked her what she'd enjoyed the most about her brief stay in Madrid. "The Prado," she replied without hesitation. "It was such a treat to see so many of the paintings I'd studied in my two art history classes in college." She and Eula had spent an entire day wandering through the world-famous museum. "I'm sorry we didn't take the time to visit Toledo, though," she told Rick.

"Yes . . . Toledo is a museum in itself," he agreed. "There are treasures of art and architecture on every corner of the city. The collection of El Grecos is un-equaled," he went on, referring to his favorite artist. "His masterpiece—*The Burial of the Count of Orgaz*—is located there."

"We should have stopped before heading to Cór-doba," Dallas said.

"If you had done that," Rick drawled softly, "we might never have met."

She raised a smiling face to his. A second later, he reached down and captured her hand. Wordlessly, he pulled her to her feet and propelled her in the direction of the dance floor.

"When you smile at me that way, I feel compelled to dance with you." His voice was gruff but full of emotion. Dallas felt a joyful glow spreading through her entire body.

The band was in the midst of a romantically lilting instrumental. With a contented sigh, Dallas relaxed against her partner's chest. Her arms seemed to have a mind of their own as they slid up around Rick's neck. In response, his hold on her tightened possessively.

"Happy, Dallas?" Rick whispered, his breath warming her skin.

"Hmm . . . incredibly." Smiling, she nuzzled her face against his jacket, wishing she could freeze this perfect moment forever in time.

"Have you forgiven me for acting like a complete idiot over Rivera?"

The silken curtain of her hair tumbled away from her face as her surprised eyes took in Rick's ruefully smiling expression. The last thing she would have expected from him was this kind of apology.

"I'm working on it," she said in a demure tone. "Rick!" she gasped when he subjected her to a tenderly wrenching bearhug.

"Let's get out of here, hmm?" Rick murmured, his

expression determined. He caught her arm and pulled her away from the dance floor. Moments later they escaped the nightclub's smoke-hung atmosphere for an enchanted garden oasis atop the hotel's roof. The night was warm as a caress, the black velvet sky aglitter with winking stars. The glowing silhouette of the massive cathedral, its lofty bell tower, and the old Alcázar palace fortress jutted upward in majestic splendor from Seville's picture-postcard skyline.

"There . . . isn't this better?" Rick asked.

"Uh-huh." She gratefully returned his kiss.

"You're amazing," Rick whispered, brushing her ear.

"I am?" Dallas queried, her heart dancing in response.

"One minute you make me so crazy I can't think straight, and the next you're all honey and warmth in my arms." He forked his fingers into the silky thickness of her hair. "In either case, I can't seem to stay away from you." He supported her head with his hands as he reclaimed her lips.

Under this exciting assault, Dallas continued to drift deliriously along in the wake of Rick's kisses.

He stroked the petal-soft skin of her throat, lingering to trace the line of her collarbone. She smiled dreamily, happiness radiating to each and every nerve ending in her body. Suddenly, Rick lifted his head. He gripped her upper arms and held her a little away from him.

"*No más, chica*—no more," he declared. "It's time to call it a night."

Dallas knew the heavenly interlude was over, but she didn't want to let go of it. She wanted to return to the warm, crushing protection of his embrace.

But she said nothing, allowing him to usher her back inside, across the heavily populated room to their table on the other side of the night club. Anita's playful wink was the only evidence that anyone had noted their prolonged absence from the table.

Roberto volunteered to drive the ladies back to their hotel, saying that it was well past his favorite patient's bedtime. Eula patted his arm affectionately and let him assist her into the waiting wheelchair.

Rick escorted them downstairs to the Palacio's main entrance and helped the doctor situate Eula on the front seat of his beige Volvo. Dallas hovered at the rear door. She felt rather dejected, thinking that her wonderful day was ending a bit anti–climactically. A citrus-scented breeze caressed her face, and she gazed up at the full, iridescent moon floating over the city like a huge, perfectly round white balloon. With a sigh, she glanced down and started to open the car door. Rick's hand on her waist arrested her, sending a familiar jolt of current to the surface of her skin.

"I'll see you tomorrow," he promised, close to her ear.

She turned her head, her hopeful eyes questioning him.

"The Hotel Argentina needs your room for an incoming tour group," he explained, his expression giving nothing away.

Surprise colored Dallas's voice. "Who told you that?"

"The manager of the hotel," Rick replied, unable to suppress his spreading grin. "He's well-paid to keep me informed."

Dallas gasped in disbelief. "Don't tell me you own the Argentina, too?!" She made a mental note to reprimand his sister, who had recommended the modest hotel. Obviously, Anita had neglected to mention that it also belonged to her brother.

Amusement glinted in Rick's indolent smoky gaze. "Sleep well, Dallas," he murmured, bending to brush her forehead with a brief, almost brotherly kiss. He couldn't have known he was asking the impossible.

When she and Eula returned to the Hotel Argentina, a friendly desk clerk handed her their key and a phone message he'd taken earlier. An agent from the Rome Music Festival Association had called to request an urgent interview with her. He'd left a number and asked that she telephone him first thing in the morning.

"Tell me I'm not dreaming, Auntie," Dallas exclaimed when they were changing into nightgowns in their room minutes later.

"You'd better get in that bed and start dreaming, kiddo," Eula warned, "otherwise you'll be too exhausted to sing tomorrow. You've had a very long and exciting day. Now it's time to sleep."

But Dallas refused to be brought down from cloud nine. Not only had she impressed Rick with her performance, she'd gotten the attention of one of the pre-eminent music festivals in Europe! It was just too good to be true!

She called Signor Ilario Bonelli early the following morning and learned, to her joy, that it was indeed true. He wanted to schedule an audition for her in Rome as soon as she was able to get there. Dallas promised to contact him when *Don Giovanni* ended and her travel arrangements were confirmed.

After a hurried breakfast and changing hotels, Dallas accompanied Anita to the cathedral for a Sunday morning service. She was still high on her news, which she happily shared with her friend.

"That's super," Anita congratulated her, "but I'm sure going to miss you." Her long face brought Dallas down to earth, making her realize suddenly her sojourn in Seville was rapidly coming to an end. The thought that she might never see Rick again acted like an instant cold shower on her buoyant mood.

From the cathedral, Dallas and Anita made their way on foot to the Barrio de Santa Cruz, with its narrow streets of whitewashed shops and old houses built around courtyards of fountains and flowers. They lunched on *paella* and *pescaíto frito*—floured fish fried in olive oil—in a small neighborhood restaurant.

"Did Rick talk to you this morning about our plans for tomorrow?" Anita inquired after she'd requested their check from a passing waiter.

"He sent a car to the Hotel Argentina for us, but I didn't see him," Dallas replied.

"He probably got tied up with that troublesome karate group," Anita said. "Anyway, we thought that since you don't have a performance tomorrow evening, the four of us could go on a picnic during the day. A friend of Rick's has a beautiful ranch northwest of the city."

"That sounds like fun," Dallas smilingly agreed. A whole day with Rick was manna from heaven, and she was eager to tell him her wonderful news. How interesting, too, that Antonio was apparently included in the outing. Perhaps Rick had warmed to Dallas's suggestion that he help his sister and her boss get together romantically after all.

Dallas had several hours to kill before leaving for the evening performance, and Anita suggested an afternoon swim in the hotel pool. When Dallas admitted she'd forgotten to pack a bathing suit, Anita cheerfully offered to lend her one.

"I can't believe you don't have any one-piece suits," Dallas complained, routing through Anita's collection in the bottom drawer of her dresser.

"Sorry, but those frumpy old-fashioned styles just aren't me. My motto is, 'if you've got it, flaunt it.' " Anita grinned.

"That's easy for you to say," Dallas retorted, "with your gorgeous tanned figure. But what about us skinny anemic types?" Dallas preferred to cover as much of her fair skin as possible.

"Hey, don't give me that," Anita chided. "You're certainly not lacking in male attention. My brother, for one, can't seem to keep his eyes off of you." Her laughing expression turned to instant dismay when she saw her friend's cheeks redden.

"Dallas, I'm sorry!" Anita exclaimed. "I shouldn't have teased you like that."

"You're exaggerating things," Dallas murmured, her gaze glancing off the other's eyes to return to the task at hand.

"I'm not and you know it," Anita declared. "I may be obsessing about my own love life at the moment, but that doesn't make me totally blind." She paused, then added, "But, hey, if you feel uncomfortable confiding in me, I can understand that. After all, he is my big brother."

Dallas kept silent, unprepared and unwilling to discuss her questionable relationship with Rick with his sister, while she herself remained stymied in the painful process of trying to fathom the significance of his lingering attention. She grimly reminded herself that a man as wealthy and accomplished as Rick, not to mention as incredibly handsome, could have practically any woman he wanted. Obviously, he felt a strong physical attraction to her, but it would be courting emotional disaster to delude herself into believing that he might be interested in more than a brief summer romance. If Rick ever got around to missing her when she and Eula departed Seville, she was convinced he would get over that in a week or two. She recalled Estela Moreno's comments about the diamond bracelet she'd lost at the Palacio Moro while having lunch with him. It certainly sounded as if the curvaceous soprano and Rick were connected in more than a professional way. Dallas felt a painful flutter in her breast whenever she pictured the two of them together.

"Don't make a big production out of a little dancing," Dallas remarked lightly, realizing it was rude to ignore Anita's overture. "You yourself said your brother is way too Spanish to ever be really interested in an American woman. And as for me," she added, her thumb pointing to her chest for emphasis, "I have my blossoming career to contend with." She shook her head resolutely. "I'm afraid I just don't have a lot of time to devote to relationships right now."

Anita mumbled something about the truth in all that. Then she helped Dallas decide on a pink and lavender paisley two-piece suit. Ten minutes later they emerged from the room attired in short terrycloth robes. En route to the elevators, they collided with Antonio Baez, looking his usual serious self.

"*Hola*, Tony," Anita greeted him. "We're going to swim."

"I can see that," her boss returned dryly. Dallas thought he seemed in a big hurry to be about his business, but Anita wouldn't let him by so easily.

"Why not change and come to the pool with us?" she invited in an enticing tone.

"*Lo siento, pero no puedo*, Anita—I'm sorry, I cannot," he said. "There's trouble, I'm afraid. I have to find your brother immediately." The young man's expression turned graver still.

"What is it, Tony? What happened?" Dallas asked.

"It appears that one of the guests has been robbed," he spoke in a subdued voice, after glancing around to insure that no one was in the vicinity to overhear their conversation.

Anita gasped. "*Qué horror*, Tony! Who?"

"You remember Señora Salazar, the wealthy woman from Buenos Aires who checked in on Wednesday?"

"Uh-huh." She nodded for him to continue.

"When Fernando suggested that she place her valuables in the safe, she declined, saying she never allows her precious jewelry out of her sight."

"How did he even know she had good stuff in the first place?" Dallas frowned.

Anita let out a low whistle. "That was easy. She was decked out in a little bit of everything when she arrived—diamonds, sapphires, a huge emerald ring—some really gaudy pieces, too."

"Gaudy or not, Anita, she's screaming her head off in the lobby. I have to locate Rick." Antonio moved off to continue his search, halting impatiently at Anita's insistent question.

"Is all her jewelry missing?"

"Only one thing, fortunately. A priceless platinum diamond necklace, she claims. She said she accidentally neglected to put it in her jewel case with the other pieces, and left it on the dresser when she went down for breakfast."

Anita groaned loudly. "Don't tell me she's blaming one of the maids!"

Antonio nodded bleakly before hurriedly vanishing down the hall.

"Darn! I hate it when something like this happens." Anita stopped in front of the elevators. She emitted a frustrated sigh of indecision. "Maybe I should go back to the room, get dressed and see if I can help out."

"That sounds like a good idea." Dallas flashed a sympathetic smile. "Don't worry about me. I can amuse myself for an hour or so."

Chapter Nine

Dallas found to her delight that she had the Palacio Moro's resort-sized pool area almost entirely to herself. And no wonder, considering the mounting heat of another smoldering summer day. A cloudless aquamarine sky stretched high above the large pool's glistening surface. Lush tropical palms shaded the recreational area, designed with marble arches and columns to resemble a fairy-tale harem pool of centuries past. Bougainvillea and hibiscus flowers contributed splashes of color to the idyllic scene.

As Dallas crossed the terra cotta clay tiles beneath the lounge chairs and wrought-iron tables, she encountered a handful of cursory glances from lazing sunbathers. Three teenaged German girls were playing in the shallows. An elderly gray-bearded tourist was laboriously engaged in swimming laps lengthwise.

Dallas stood at the pool's edge and gazed down into the clear inviting water, debating whether she should test its temperature or settle for a vacant chair nearby. When the boisterous teens climbed out and raced to the poolside bar, the serene water seemed preferable to sweating in the scorching heat of the Iberian afternoon. Grateful for the sunscreen provided by Anita, Dallas decided to try the water.

After kicking off her sandals and shedding her terry coverup, she deposited her towel on a chair. *"Gracias,"* she said, accepting an air-filled plastic float from a grinning pool attendant, an olive-skinned youth whose eyes had instantly caught the arrival of the pretty blond.

Dallas slipped slowly into the water, which chilled her warm skin. Shivering momentarily, she submerged once, shook her dripping hair back, then lifted herself onto the raft. Careful to stay out of the swimmer's path, she paddled briefly around the large pool. Presently, with a contented sigh, she put her head down, lazily making a mental note not to fall asleep. The last thing she needed was to be late getting to the theater.

Dozing languorously, the bare skin of her back and limbs heated by the blazing sun, she began once again to wish that she could freeze her life just where it was at this moment in time. What a dreamer she'd become, she mused, grimacing inwardly while forming a handsome picture of Rick in her mind's eye.

She always thought she would eventually fall in

love with and marry a man somewhat like her professor father—someone intelligent, generous, honest and
secure. She wondered what it would be like to be married to a man like Rick. He was successful, certainly,
and represented financial security. But that volatile
Latin temperament of his would undoubtedly make
life a rollercoaster ride of endless ups and downs. Just
thinking about him made her dizzy, she reflected ruefully. Still, the probability that she would never see
him again once she left Spain gnawed at her serenity.
She tried to convince herself that it was the thought
of leaving Seville—which she had grown to love—
that was disturbing her. In an attempt to dispel this
troubling reverie, she recalled her conversation with
Ilario Bonelli. The Italian agent had been so impressed
with her performance that he knew there were several
juicy roles she would be considered for during the
Rome auditions, including Musetta in *La Bohème*.

Sometime later, a nearby splash stirred Dallas into
lifting her head to look around the pool; a glance
around revealed that the elderly tourist was gone. As
she lowered her head to resume her catnap, she spotted
a long, dark-suited figure traveling like an underwater
torpedo in the direction of her raft. She only had time
for a gasp, followed by a panicky squeal, before her
float was roughly capsized. Dallas splashed gracelessly
into the sparkling water's cool depths.

After choking and sputtering her way to the surface,
she emerged face to face with a grinning Rick. His
brown arms whipped around her like steel bands,
crushing her to his wide muscled chest.

"Didn't your mother ever tell you how dangerous it is to swim alone?" He arched an eyebrow, gray eyes laughing at her.

Dallas's impulse was to fling her arms around his neck and cover his wet face with fervent kisses. Instead, she feigned irritation, saying: "I wasn't swimming . . . until now." She shoved ineffectually at his glistening bronze shoulders.

Rick whipped his gleaming dark hair back from his forehead. He relaxed his hold on her, starting to say something. Taking instant advantage of his unguarded stance, Dallas pushed off the floor of the pool, lifted her hands and flattened them on top of his head. Summoning all her strength, she dunked him once, hard. While he was still underwater, she turned and swam frantically in the direction of one of the ladders. To her dismay, she didn't even get within splashing range of the steps before Rick had captured her ankle in his powerful grip. He pulled her inexorably back to him.

"Rick! No!" Dallas cried out, breathless, knowing he would get even.

"You asked for it, *bruja!*" he roared before dunking her in retaliation. She had scarcely regained the water's surface before his arm snaked around her waist. He yanked her to him once again.

"You're not getting away that easily," he drawled, a wicked smile curving his mouth.

"Stop, Rick . . . please! You'll drown me!" Her hands flew to his shoulders.

"I may do just that if you don't settle down and kiss me," he threatened in a low growl.

Dallas's strident protestations melted before the fire in his eyes. She surrendered, without a thought that they might have poolside witnesses.

"Where did you get this swim suit, *chica?*" he asked in a husky voice against her cheek. "I like it," he said.

"Anita lent it to me. . . ." Dallas experienced the seeking pressure of Rick's kiss again. But mentioning his sister brought her back to reality, albeit with great reluctance. Heart thudding swiftly, she interrupted the kiss by twisting her head.

"My sister always did have good taste," he drawled with a grin. His narrowed gaze intently studied Dallas's face for long seconds. She couldn't decide if the burning she felt was from the afternoon sun overhead or his prolonged scrutiny.

"Speaking of Anita," Dallas said, suddenly remembering why her friend hadn't come with her to the pool, "is there any news about that woman's diamond necklace?"

"Uh-huh." Rick lifted his hand to send his fingers roaming over Dallas's face, slow and exploringly, like a blind man reading Braille. Her features were delicately classic, her long-lashed eyes the color of fine blue-and-white Chinese porcelain.

Distracted by his touch, she was having difficulty concentrating on speech, but she managed another question. "Don't tell me the maid did it?"

"Okay . . . I won't tell you that."

"Rick, be serious! Did they find the necklace?"

He sighed, halting his tantalizing exploration of her skin. "It never left the woman's room," he explained.

"Antonio located it in the trash can next to the dresser. It must have slipped in, and the silly woman was so hysterical she neglected to check there."

The teenaged girls chose that moment to reestablish their original claim on the shallow end of the pool. Giggling and hollering, they splashed in, sending a chilling spray of water shooting at Dallas and Rick.

"Come on . . . let's go," he grumbled, releasing his willing prisoner. He pushed her in the direction of the ladder and followed her there. She made a dash for her towel as soon as she emerged dripping from the pool, and wrapped the terrycloth around her like a sarong, averting shy eyes from Rick's sweeping gaze.

"Hiding yourself from me is pointless, *pequeña*," he informed her in a deep caressing tone. "We both know it's only a matter of time before this thing between us evolves to its natural culmination."

Dallas blushed scarlet, stung by what she perceived to be an arrogant, presumptuous remark. "Just because I let you kiss me doesn't mean you own me," she retorted in an agitated voice.

Rick's features hardened into granite as he stood tall before her in black swim trunks. His narrowed eyes glittered as he glared down at her. "I don't know what you imagine I meant," he said in exasperation, "but I thought we were making headway."

"I—I don't understand what you want from me, Rick," Dallas declared, feeling sick to her stomach that this conversation was taking place.

"I believe what *you* want is at issue here," he came back at her.

Her brain was whirling with doubt and confusion. "Well, of course, I want us to be friends," she blurted impulsively.

His incredulous grunt startled her. "Is that what we've been doing here? Making *friends* with each other?" he said, a sarcastic bite to his tone.

Wounded, Dallas stiffened. "You have your work and I have mine, Rick. Friendship is about all I can handle at the moment. Besides, Eula and I are leaving the day after the last performance of *Don Giovanni*."

"Why?" he demanded, surprise slashing his face. "What's the big rush?"

Dallas quickly told him about her conversation with Ilario Bonelli. "I . . . I thought you'd be happy for me," she ended on a dismal note when Rick's expression remained dark.

"What do you think I am, Dallas? A saint?" He scowled as she continued to gape at him, pain and bewilderment in her moist eyes.

With jaw clenched, Rick tossed his head to the side, as if suddenly unable to bear the look he had inspired on her face. His chest rose and fell heavily while he wrestled with his own indecision. "I'm sorry, Dallas," he said brusquely, raking a hand through his slick, damp hair. "I do congratulate you, and I hope you'll be very successful with your career." He turned abruptly, leaving her to miserably wonder why there didn't appear to have been a single thread of warmth or sincerity in his stark tone.

Chapter Ten

Dallas stumbled sleepily around the room, trying in vain not to awaken her aunt. Her bright mood of the previous day had evaporated, and although Sunday's performance had been another smashing success, her spirits refused to rise.

"I'm sorry, Auntie . . . I didn't mean to wake you." She smiled apologetically as Eula shifted in her bed, yawning broadly.

"That's okay, hon. I got enough shut-eye." Her glance took in her niece's flattering outfit of slim-fitting blue jeans and a long-sleeved plaid shirt beneath a tan cotton vest. A pair of cognac leather boots, borrowed from Anita the day before, hugged Dallas's calves. "Who all's going on this picnic?" Eula wanted to know.

"It was supposed to be just four of us," Dallas replied grimly, "but somehow Miguel and Estela got included at the last minute. Anita didn't elaborate on it." Dallas stepped to the dresser, ran a hurried comb through her hair and cast a final critical eye at her reflection, one hand lifting to adjust the collar of her blouse.

"I bet Rick invited them," Eula suggested, propping her elbow on a pillow.

"Invited her, maybe," Dallas retorted, unable to disguise the petulance in her voice.

"If I didn't know better, Dall, I'd say you were jealous of that woman." Eula's hazel eyes twinkled speculatively.

Dallas's mouth dropped open before she hastily protested. "Jealous of her? My voice is every bit as—"

"Not *professional* jealousy," Eula interrupted her.

"You mean because of Rick?" Dallas demanded, glancing around for her purse. "As far as I'm concerned, those two can have each other," she stated vehemently, grabbing her bag off the dresser.

"Well, do try to have fun, sweetie," Eula suggested.

"I'm planning on it," Dallas chirped with forced gaiety, bending to kiss the older woman's cheek. "You're sure you'll be okay without me?" she asked belatedly.

"Don't worry about me. Roberto is coming by to pick me up between ten and ten-thirty. We're going to visit the Alcázar and an art museum he's particularly fond of, and then we're having lunch." Eula's happy smile made Dallas instantly envious.

* * *

The drive through the city then northwest on a narrow highway took more than an hour. In other circumstances, Dallas would have thoroughly enjoyed the stunning scenery: distant mountain peaks, green and yellow grasslands broken at intervals by sloping olive groves, scattered herds of grazing cattle, and tiny white stucco houses decorated with black iron balconies and gardens teeming with flowers.

Estela's mood proved worse than her young rival's, particularly when she was forced to sit in the back of the Mercedes when Miguel chose the passenger window seat for himself, and insisted that Dallas join him up front. When the prima donna complained, Miguel had merely laughed, protesting that his legs were certainly longer than hers, and he refused to be cramped on his first day off in many months.

Rick drove swiftly and silently, seemingly unaware of the tense feminine figure at his right. It was impossible for Dallas to avoid the warm imprint of his side without overcrowding Miguel, though certainly the older man would have had no objection. As it was, she brushed against both men often, whenever the luxury car swerved along its winding path.

Anita was delighted to be next to Antonio, who seemed more relaxed than usual. She and Miguel kept the conversation flowing throughout the drive, but Dallas breathed a sigh of relief when Rick turned the car onto a bumpy dirt road. Within minutes, a long row of stables materialized through the glaring haze of another hot summer day.

While Rick conversed with several rugged-looking

ranch hands about suitable horses for his party, Dallas wandered alone through the stable yard, savoring the aroma of horses and hay. For a moment she felt free from all tension and anxiety, reminded of the carefree summers of her youth spent on a cousin's farm in west Texas. She shaded her eyes with one hand to survey the stretch of dry green pasture beyond a dusty corral encircled by a white fence. The southern sky was pale blue and heavily dappled with clouds, with some ominous gray layers off in the distance.

Presently, Anita hailed her, and Dallas hastened back to the stables.

"How well do you ride?" Rick inquired, his tone coolly polite.

Dallas felt a painful tightening around her heart at his continued aloofness. "I'm average, I guess," she replied. The other four had already mounted and begun a trail away from the corral.

"Hurry up, you two," Anita called over her shoulder.

One of the ranch hands approached, leading a sleek black filly who elegantly tossed her head. The mahogany curtain of her mane whipped like a flag in the parched breeze.

"She's a beauty!" Dallas exclaimed, running her hand down the animal's velvety neck. "What's her name?" she queried with a smile, determined to ignore Rick's mood.

"La Duquesa Negra," the smiling young man replied, before handing the horse's reins to Rick, who translated for Dallas.

" 'The Black Duchess.' Think you can handle her? She's a feisty little thing," he drawled.

"I reckon I can try," Dallas murmured, inserting her booted foot into the stirrup. A breath caught in her chest as she felt Rick's hands circling her waist. He assisted her effortlessly into the worn leather saddle. With pulses fluttering wildly, she managed a breathless *"gracias"* when he passed her the reins.

"De nada, señorita," he said with quiet formality, pausing to adjust the stirrups to support her feet. He was wearing snake-skin boots and black jeans. His full sleeved gaucho shirt was white and opened at his throat, revealing a dark thatch of hair. As she studied him surreptitiously, Dallas was bluntly reminded of their interlude in the hotel swimming pool the day before. Her skin grew warmer, and her jittery gaze darted to Rick's face. He looked up at her, those insolent gray eyes shattering her fragile composure. It alarmed her to find his expression so taunting and sure, as if he could read her mind and knew well the devastating effect he had upon her.

Feeling a desperate need to be free of his mocking regard, Dallas wheeled her horse and urged the Duchess into a trot toward the sun-baked dirt path which the others, now nearly a quarter of a mile away, had followed. She dared a glance over her shoulder and saw Rick quickly mount his horse, a sorrel-colored, powerfully-built Arabian stallion named Diablo. With a tap of his heel and a low verbal command, Rick sent his horse charging after the female duo.

Heart thumping, Dallas hesitated only a split second

before she gave one kick of her boots and sent the Duchess plunging forward over the flatland, her hooves pounding in an exhilarating gallop. Rick's stallion overtook the graceful filly with ease. Dallas glanced sideways. She blushed, decidedly shaken by the amused mask of triumph on Rick's tawny face. His expression suggested that she was free to try and run from him, but he would always be able to catch her, whenever he chose to do so.

They slowed their horses to a comfortable lope, then to an ambling walk as they neared the others, who had reached a small cluster of trees. The scent of wildflowers was in the air, and birds sang happily as the midday sun pierced the clouded sky.

"So, *chica*, you reveal another talent," Rick drawled, his hands firm on the aggressive stallion's reins. The Duchess, intimidated by Diablo's proximity, whinnied softly and nervously tossed her shining mane.

Dallas looked into Rick's charcoal eyes and noted a smiling hint of approval. *Heavens! This man's moods are as mercurial as the Iberian weather!* Although she tried not to, she couldn't help but respond to him. Her lips twitched in an upward curve. "I *was* born and raised in Texas. Besides, with a little practice, anybody can ride a horse," she said, dismissing the compliment. The next instant their attention was drawn to the others when they heard a female voice clucking in anger.

"Well . . . almost anybody," Dallas amended, barely able to suppress a giggle at the sight of Estela pushing herself to her feet and furiously dusting the seat of her expensive linen slacks. Apparently the soprano was not as accustomed to horseback riding as the others.

Dallas watched a grinning Miguel swing off his horse and approach his leading lady, who was now glaring murderously at her stationary steed. "Leave me alone," Estela snapped, but Miguel ignored her words and helped her to remount.

"Try holding on this time, *amor*," he instructed, inclining his head to receive a stream of unladylike Castilian curses.

After more than an hour of riding, perspiration trickled freely down Dallas's back, making her cotton shirt clingy and damp. Still, she continued to savor the country air, thick with the scent of grassy meadows. Estela, on the other hand, complained incessantly, causing the others to wonder what had prompted her to come along in the first place.

Anita halted the group in a shaded area along a narrow stream, dismounted, and began to unload a saddlebag laden with cheeses, bread and fresh fruit. Antonio produced bottles of water from his bag. Everyone collapsed wearily to the ground, leaving the horses tethered to some low-branched trees several yards away. Conversation was at a minimum, and the ravenous riders consumed their picnic lunch in a matter of minutes.

Dallas was absorbed in helping Anita pack away the remnants of their meal when she heard Estela's enticing murmur. "Walk with me, Ricardo?" the soprano asked Rick as he stood at the bank of the stream.

"Of course, Estelita," he replied, welcoming her silk-adorned arm as she entwined it about his.

Dallas shut out the sight of the splendid couple they made, but she winced visibly at the pain caused by the abrupt lurch of her heart. She'd noticed earlier that Estela was wearing an expensive diamond tennis bracelet on her right wrist. Dallas wondered again, as she had that morning, if Rick had given it to her to replace her canary diamond bracelet that had not been found.

Presently, Anita and Antonio slipped off, leaving Dallas to share the solitude and the shade with Miguel and the six resting horses. With a sigh, she sat on the ground and leaned back against a tree, a few feet away from where Miguel was reclining, palms beneath his head, hat shielding his face. He appeared to be napping peacefully.

Pushing his hat from his face quite suddenly, Miguel raised himself on an elbow and turned to survey Dallas. She blinked at him, surprised to see that his usually dancing eyes were serious and faintly sad.

"It seems that you and I share the same ship, eh, Dallas?" He slanted her a crooked smile. "Isn't that one of your American expressions?"

"You mean we're 'in the same boat'?" she queried, frowning slightly, at a loss to his meaning.

Miguel nodded. "You do not need to pretend with me. Love is a gentle blue flame in your eyes." He shook his head dismally. "And I have my beautiful Estela to torment me. We're a fine pair, hmm?"

Dallas didn't know which had astounded her more:

Miguel's assumption concerning her feelings for Rick, or his revelation that he was in love with his temperamental prima donna. Unable to confirm what she had yet to admit to herself, she focused on Miguel's problem. "How long have you loved her, Miguel?" she asked quietly.

"Forever, it seems." His voice was flat. "Unfortunately, I have realized it too late, and now it is all rather hopeless."

"But why?"

He sighed heavily. "It's a long story."

"I have plenty of time," Dallas prompted, smiling.

Miguel took a deep breath before launching into his recitation. "Many years ago, Estelita and I were lovers. She begged me to marry her, but I was stubborn and ambitious, and dedicated to establishing my career in the music world. Realizing her talent, I encouraged her to pursue her career as well, hoping thus to assuage my guilt for rejecting her, I suppose. I also believed she would find someone else, marry and be happy, and I could continue my grand and noble pursuits unencumbered."

He made a wry face before going on. "Of course, Estela did nothing of the sort. Spurred on by what seemed to be an obsession to prove to me that she did not need me, or any other man in order to be fulfilled and successful, she began to study and practice. Before long, her career was progressing as fruitfully as my own. Eventually, and perhaps inevitably, they coincided several years ago and we found ourselves working closely together." He paused, his expression grave.

"I have learned—and sadly, too late—that I have always loved her and always will . . . even though bitterness has made her somewhat disagreeable."

Sympathy abounded in Dallas's heart for the poor man. "But, Miguel, if you would just tell Estela how you feel," she suggested hopefully.

"I tried to do that when we first began working together, but she acted so cold. She insisted on a purely businesslike relationship, saying that her career was the only important thing in her life. I suppose I deserve her scorn now, after the way I treated her years ago."

"Don't be so hard on yourself, Miguel," Dallas rejoined. "Everybody makes mistakes and choices they regret later on."

"True . . . and some find it difficult, if not impossible, to forgive. Even if Estelita were to forgive me, that would not guarantee the return of her affection . . . especially if there was another man in her life." He halted, eyeing Dallas thoughtfully.

To her immense relief, she was saved from having to respond by the return of Anita and Antonio, hand in hand. Dallas got to her feet, bent down to dust her jeans, and hoped that Miguel wouldn't notice the twin blotches of pink on her hot cheeks.

"Where's my brother?" Anita demanded, her green eyes sparkling with barely-contained excitement. Miguel shrugged and resumed his lazy recumbent position on the grass.

"He and Estela went for a walk," Dallas supplied, hoping she had sounded sufficiently indifferent.

"I wish they would hurry up and get back here,"

Anita declared. Her rapturous gaze lifted to Antonio's curiously smiling face.

"Here they come now," Dallas said, sighting Rick and the soprano about fifty yards away, arms still entwined.

"Terrific," Anita chirped, waving and gesturing for them to hasten their approach.

"What are you jumping up and down for, *hermanita*?" Rick drawled inquiringly minutes later.

"I have big news, and I wanted to tell all of you at once," Anita exclaimed.

"Well, what is it?" her brother demanded, feigning irritation.

"We're engaged!" The radiant brunette grasped her boss's arm with uninhibited glee. To his credit, the usually solemn young Spaniard looked properly pleased himself.

The next several moments passed with a flurry of surprised congratulations, hugs, kisses and backslapping. Her and Miguel's problems temporarily forgotten, Dallas advanced to embrace Anita warmly when Rick's deep voice halted the merriment.

"It has just occurred to me that there's been a rather serious omission here," he began, his frowning gaze shifting from Antonio to Anita.

"What is it, Rick?" Antonio inquired, matching the other's mock serious tone.

"You've neglected to obtain my permission for this marriage, *amigo*."

"That's true," Anita interrupted the men. "Actually, Tony wanted to formally ask you for my hand, but I wouldn't let him." She grinned. "I was afraid you might refuse."

"Refuse?" Rick snorted. "I've been trying to get rid of you for years!"

For all his play at being difficult, he was clearly delighted with his sister's news. And even Estela's well-wishing had an uncharacteristic sincerity about it. Miguel, too, was happy for the beaming couple. He asked Antonio when the wedding would take place.

"As soon as possible," the young man replied.

"Ah, you are impatient to start a family, eh?"

"No, I am impatient to get Anita out of the hotel!" Antonio retorted, suffering a reproachful glare from his lovely bride-to-be.

"Anita, *querida*, you know I am only joking. You're the best assistant manager in all of Spain," he assured her, slipping his arm affectionately around her waist. "Nevertheless, you are fired," he finished smugly. Anita chuckled, shaking her head resignedly. The three men roared their laughter.

"Why not look on the bright side, *amiga*," Dallas broke in, her wide gaze reflecting her friend's happiness. "Think of all the spare time you'll have for retail therapy." She winked at Anita who nodded, giggling.

"That sounds suspiciously like 'shopping,'" Rick translated with a grin.

Antonio groaned, clutching his forehead in a gesture of dismay. "*Dios mío!* I'll be in the poorhouse within a year."

"But it will be well worth it, eh, *hombre*?" Miguel smiled philosophically.

"*Sí, absolutamente,*" Antonio agreed.

* * *

The atmosphere surrounding the journey back to the stables was subdued compared to the jubilation following Anita's announcement. Each rider seemed pensive and lost in thought. The sky appeared to mirror this mood change, for by the time they reached the stable yard, black clouds were hovering threateningly over the dry flatland.

"We'd better hurry," Anita exclaimed. "It looks like it's going to storm any minute." Her suggestion was as unnecessary as her weather report, because most of the group were already assisting the two ranch hands in returning the nervous animals to their stalls.

Only Estela remained glued to her saddle, glowering and impatiently awaiting help from one of the men. Dallas emerged from the stables as Rick was approaching to assist the sour-faced singer. With no warning, a blinding streak of lightning forked through the dark churning sky overhead, as a deafening rumble of thunder sounded.

Startled, Dallas gasped, reflexively gripping the swinging stable door with white-knuckled fingers. The scene before her unfolded in a horrifying tapestry of slow motion. Estela screamed, a high-pitched sound of surprise and terror. Her chestnut gelding, the oldest and most docile of the six horses they'd been riding, reared and whinnied shrilly. Its forelegs raked the air perilously close to Rick's head as he fought to grab the reins and Estela at the same time. His arm circled her waist and hauled her from the saddle, then he shoved her away from the horse who continued its two-legged dance, hooves swirling dust everywhere.

Another explosive thunderclap erupted, further inciting the panic-stricken animal. Dallas unfroze and dashed forward to enfold the crouched, sobbing Estela in her arms. Estela's face remained hidden in her hands, but Dallas's wide, frightened eyes never left Rick. He had a firm hold on the gelding's reins and was agilely avoiding its flailing legs while he tried to calm the horse by murmuring low and soothingly in Spanish.

Dallas was kneeling, paralyzed in the dirt, her arms tightly hugging a tearful Estela. Terrified for Rick, Dallas's breath remained trapped in her lungs for so long she began to feel lightheaded. She vaguely heard the sound of others running from the stalls. She saw Rick glare at Antonio and the two young ranch hands who were racing forward to help. The trio stopped short and slowly backed away so as not to alarm the gradually settling horse. Moments later, Rick was patting the animal's sweating neck and leading him toward the waiting men.

By this time Miguel and Anita, who'd been witnessing the harrowing scene from a distance, dashed forward to help Estela and Dallas to their feet. The conductor, his dark eyes concerned, took Estela against his chest and ran a soothing hand over her sleek black hair.

"I'm fine," Dallas murmured when Anita began to cluck over her.

"Are you sure you're okay?" Anita questioned her frowningly. "You look pale as a ghost."

"I'm not the one who almost got trampled," Dallas said, disturbed by the tremor in her own voice. "Maybe you'd better check on your brother," she managed hoarsely. Rick was standing several yards away wiping his glistening forehead with a handkerchief and talking to Antonio.

"I'll do that," Anita agreed, "but he appears to be all in one piece." She walked quickly toward the men.

Dazed, Dallas wandered to the nearby corral and leaned against one of its dusty boards. Her legs had begun to quiver violently. Her heart pounded as her stomach reeled with nausea as she considered how close Rick had come to being badly injured. She watched him now. Grinning broadly, he strolled over to where Miguel stood with Estela. The beautiful soprano left the older man's comforting embrace to raise her tear-streaked face to Rick, who said something and welcomed her when she moved to hug him in apparent gratitude.

Absorbing this scene, Dallas felt sicker still. With a painful stab of realization that tore at her heart, she recognized and accepted her condition in that moment. Miguel had recognized it before she, so dense and narrow-minded had she become, letting her career consume her life. *She had fallen in love with Rick.* She shuddered with the chill that this discovery left in its wake. Then another roar of thunder rumbled above, and suddenly the sky opened up.

Chapter Eleven

"*S*ube el telón en cinco minutos*! Curtain in five minutes!"

Dallas heard the now-familiar announcement through the excited backstage din. She hastily applied the finishing touches to her makeup. If possible, this final performance was going even better than all the others, and already the city's music critics and opera buffs had agreed that Maestro Miguel Rivera had achieved his greatest success to date.

Gripped by a hollow feeling of sadness, Dallas prepared for the last act. She had grown fond of so many of the cast and crew, she would miss working with them. Of course, there would be a lot more to miss about her stay in Seville than the lovely city and the opera participants—much more, she reflected grimly.

She grew cold and morose whenever she thought about Rick. The last time she'd seen him was the night of the picnic, when he'd deposited her, Anita and Antonio at the hotel. Estela had remained a tearful bundle of nerves on the return drive into the city, made longer because of the unexpected summer storm. When Miguel had suggested taking her home, she'd clung to Rick, who finally decided she should see Roberto Hidalgo. The doctor would surely prescribe a tranquilizer for her.

"She obviously doesn't want me around," Miguel had muttered to Dallas as they all stood uncertainly by the car in front of the hotel. He bid everyone a curt *"adiós"* and departed in a taxi. Estela had promptly burst into tears.

"I'm driving her to the hospital," Rick had told the others, and seconds later his Mercedes was out of sight.

The following morning Dallas discovered that Rick had once again left town on business. At first she felt despondent when Anita said that he would be in Madrid through the weekend. Then she decided it was definitely for the best. She couldn't have borne a casual goodbye kiss from him.

Eula didn't seem too enthusiastic when Dallas asked her to come to Rome, but she'd reluctantly agreed, and Dallas called the airline to make two reservations. Then she phoned Ilario Bonelli to give him their arrival time. It was done. She could leave unceremoniously the morning after the final performance, resigned to never seeing Rick Santana again, and hope that the old adage "out of sight, out of mind" might work a miracle on her broken heart.

She ventured out one last time to Calle Sierpes, returning to the shop where she and Anita saw the exquisite Lladró bride and groom. She asked a smiling sales clerk to box and wrap the figurine as a wedding present, confident that Anita would be thrilled with the gift.

Then Dallas hurried to catch a cab to take her to the theater, pausing only briefly to gaze in the window of a particularly elegant jewelry store. There were brightly glittering rings, pendants, bracelets, earrings and brooches of every description. Spotting a small butterfly decorated with sapphires and diamonds, Dallas recalled the gold gemstone pin that Henri Thevenot had given to Teresa. She remembered that Teresa had mentioned her boyfriend worked in a tourist shop on Calle Sierpes. Wondering how he could afford such an expensive item, Dallas decided maybe it was a piece of costume jewelry, although the sparkling stones had certainly appeared genuine.

The final act of *Don Giovanni* was better than Miguel could have hoped for. After a prolonged standing ovation, Dallas retreated to the dressing room with the knowledge that she had done her best. She had accepted the great challenge and met it head-on. Bemoaning the fact that she didn't feel very happy about it, she dropped wearily onto a stool in front of the long mirror. She removed her dark wig and began the tedious chore of cleansing her face of its thick layer of theatrical makeup.

The room was curiously empty, because Miguel had invited everyone to an adjacent restaurant for a final celebration, and most had decided to go in costume. Dallas planned to change into street clothes, grab a taxi and be in bed by one o'clock. The flight she had booked for herself and Eula was scheduled to depart for Rome at eleven-thirty the following morning.

Miguel had been disappointed, but encouraging, when Dallas had confided her plans to him.

"Our loss will be the great gain of the Rome Festival," he had said sincerely. "But remember, *querida*, there will always be a place for you with this company as long as I am here." She'd thanked him profusely before hugging him.

Hearing the rattle of the dressing room door, Dallas's gaze shifted to see Teresa's smiling reflection in the long mirror. "Hey . . . aren't you going to the restaurant?" she asked the pretty redhead.

"*Sí*, but I wish to change from my costume." The girl's smile became sad. "I'm so sorry you are not coming with us tonight, Dallas. I will miss you."

"Same here," Dallas murmured, turning to clasp Teresa's outstretched hand. "I just hate long goodbyes," she sighed. "That's the main reason I'm skipping the after-party. And my aunt and I are going to have a very full day tomorrow."

Teresa changed quickly while Dallas continued to clean her face at the mirror. They chatted about the performance, agreeing that it was the best of a highly successful run. Teresa told Dallas that the company would be doing *La Traviata* in the fall, and she regretted that she would miss it, since her fiancé was taking her to France where they were to be married.

After hurriedly applying lipstick, Teresa reached for her purse and fished inside. She approached Dallas and grabbed her hand impulsively, turning it palm up and depositing a shining object.

Puzzled, Dallas glanced down, incredulity in her voice when she realized what it was. "Teresa! I can't take this. Isn't it the pin Henri gave you?" It was the golden butterfly brooch covered with diamonds, rubies and emeralds.

"Yes, but I want you to have it," Teresa replied. "He has given me other things as well." She smiled. "You must take it as a memento of our friendship."

"But it's way too expensive—"

"No, no, the stones are not real," Teresa said, a note of apology in her voice.

"Did Henri tell you that?" Dallas queried, feeling a flash of suspicion her brain couldn't quite comprehend.

"No, but they cannot be real. Henri could not afford to buy such things." The Spanish girl fumbled in her purse again, producing a plump black felt pouch. When she emptied the contents on the makeup counter, Dallas gasped in amazement. There were at least a dozen small items of jewelry: rings, pins and earrings, all sparkling with the quality and brilliance of genuine stones.

"They are very beautiful, yes?" Teresa exclaimed, smiling.

"Yes, indeed . . ." *And very real, I'd be willing to bet*, Dallas thought to herself.

Something was wrong somewhere. Her mind grappled for an explanation. What had she heard at the hotel? Anita had mentioned some newspaper articles about a growing epidemic of robberies in Seville. She recalled Rick's friend's wife, whose jewelry had been stolen from their home. Could there be a connection here? But how awful for Teresa if Henri were somehow involved in those crimes. Surely it wasn't possible, Dallas argued with her suspicions. Nevertheless, she was certain these pieces were made of precious metals and genuine gemstones. Her grandfather had been a jeweler for over thirty years, and she'd spent a lot of time visiting him at the store where he worked in Fort Worth. He always enjoyed teaching her about the different colored stones and ways to distinguish the natural ones from synthetics.

"I wish they were real," Teresa chirped gaily. "But Henri makes very little money at the shop, and his apartment rent is quite high."

"That may be, but I'm positive this is good jewelry," Dallas insisted, examining one small earring. A square emerald green stone was surrounded by winking diamonds. "Look here . . . this one's stamped on the back. Isn't that '18K'?"

Teresa bent to inspect the minute marking. "*Sí-sí* . . . it is," she replied in a hushed tone. "*Madre mía* . . . what does this mean?"

"It means you are both in trouble," came a tight male voice, heavily accented and undeniably hostile.

Startled, Dallas and Teresa twisted simultaneously to see Henri Thevenot standing by the door. To Dallas, the Frenchman's sullen face and unfriendly manner seemed more pronounced than usual. Clad totally in black, he'd slipped soundlessly into the dressing room while they were engrossed in their scrutiny of the mysterious jewelry.

"Henri! What are you doing here?" Teresa demanded, nervously returning the tiny articles to her pouch.

"Didn't I tell you not to show those to anyone until we left Seville?" he snapped at her. "You just couldn't wait, eh?"

"I'm sorry, Henri," his fiancée whimpered meekly. "I didn't think you would mind if I showed them to Dallas."

"After I told you exactly how much I minded the other day—when I discovered you had shown her the butterfly!" He waved his hand in a gesture of disgust.

"I—I forgot." Teresa's low voice trembled.

"You've ruined everything with your stupidity," he hissed, prompting Dallas to intervene with spirit.

"Calm down, Henri. There's no need to talk to her that way. You're acting like the jewelry was stolen or something," she baited him, instantly regretting her words.

"Stolen!?" Teresa cried.

"What do you think, *imbécile*? You believe I make

money in that miserable shop on Calle Sierpes?" He sneered, his black eyes glittering angrily.

Dallas watched as fear and confusion appeared in Teresa's face. It was obvious the girl had been totally ignorant of her fiancé's extracurricular activities.

As for Dallas, she was now convinced beyond a doubt that Henri was somehow involved in the string of jewel heists which had plagued Seville for the past several weeks. How incredibly coincidental that Teresa would try to give her one of the pieces that had been stolen from Rick's friend's wife! If only it had clicked in her brain earlier, Dallas berated herself, when she'd first seen the butterfly. She might have confided her suspicions to Rick and had Henri investigated.

Suddenly another thought skyrocketed in her head. As far as she knew, Estela's missing bracelet had never surfaced at the hotel, the theater or anywhere else. Dallas's curiosity got the better of her, and she couldn't resist confronting Thevenot about it. "You didn't happen to recently come across a canary diamond tennis bracelet, did you, Henri?" she interrogated him.

She caught and held her breath as a contemptuous scowl distorted his face. With a dangerous glint in his gaze, he stared at her for long seconds. Then with a half-smile, he reached in his shirt pocket to produce another small black pouch. Turning it with one hand, he deposited its contents in the palm of his other hand. "You mean this bracelet?" He wore a conceited smirk.

"I did not think Señorita Moreno would miss it . . . she has so many beautiful things."

"You took it from her dressing room, didn't you?" Dallas accused.

His unpleasant smile widened. "It was so very simple," he bragged. "During the rehearsals and performances these dressing rooms are often empty." He glanced down at the golden coil of brilliant yellow stones cupped in his hand. "This will fetch enough on the black market for a first-class honeymoon," he added, turning to Teresa. "Come on," he ordered impatiently. He stuffed the bracelet back in his pocket. "We have to get out of here—"

"*Ladrón*! You expect me to go with you—a thief!?" she declared, her voice leaping an octave. She hurled a volley of abusive Spanish at him, amber eyes sparking.

Dallas stood motionless, trying to remain calm amidst the duo's explosive battle. Her stomach was tight with distress, while her brain worked to translate their heated words and gesticulations. She could tell that Henri was demanding that his fiancée accompany him, but it was equally obvious that Teresa was adamantly refusing to do so, outraged to learn that her beloved was nothing but a common thief.

Dallas's nails dug painfully into her palms as she clenched her fists, wishing this nightmare would end. Summoning strength, she stepped between the two combatants, motioning for them to cease. Normally, she would have been hesitant to get involved in such a fiery display, but now, she had grown fearful that the situation was rapidly escalating out of control.

"I said that's enough, you two!" she repeated forcefully, after her first unheeded attempt to silence them.

Henri was livid, his teeth bared, his nostrils flaring. Angry tears had begun to stream down Teresa's cheeks, and Dallas could see the poor girl shaking with reaction.

"If you can't understand Spanish, Henri, perhaps my English will convince you," Dallas said icily, facing the man. "She has no desire to go with you, so why don't you just leave . . . before I decide to call the police."

"That would be most unwise, *mademoiselle*," Henri said slowly, a nasty expression embedded in his face.

Dallas's heart started to race. It was courting disaster to provoke him too much, she reflected belatedly, feeling a stirring of fear. What if he had a weapon and tried to use it on them?

"Look, Henri, we'll leave the authorities out of this if you'll just go," she lied.

"Sí, váyase!" Teresa spat at him.

"I should get rid of you, you know," he snarled at Dallas. "My partners, they would, if they were here now."

"Ha! *Naturalmente* you have help with these crimes!" Teresa jeered tearfully. "You are not enough the man to make the success alone!" Her English was deteriorating in her hysteria.

"Mon Dieu! You—you little—!" The Frenchman's

features contorted with rage. He lunged for Teresa, brutally shoving Dallas aside.

"Don't you touch me!" Teresa shrieked in her own language, taking a frightened step backwards and coming up against the makeup counter.

Ranting in French, Henri grabbed her right arm with bruising strength. He raised his other hand, clearly intending to slap Teresa senseless, but Dallas had recovered her balance and came at him like a ferocious lioness protecting her only cub. She grabbed his wrist with both hands, at the same moment sending her right foot in a sharp kick to his leg.

"You bully! Leave her alone!" Dallas shouted, silently praying that someone nearby would hear the commotion. Of all the times for everyone to have deserted the theater! Panic gripped her heart because she knew she would not be able to thwart Henri for very much longer. He wasn't a large man, but he was young and extremely strong. Her kick had glanced off his leg with little effect save the kindling of his fury.

Deciding he couldn't hope to succeed with his rebellious fiancée while her friend remained to interfere, Henri released Teresa abruptly and turned on Dallas, a menacing glow in his lethal gaze.

"I have had enough of your meddling, *mademoiselle*." With a smirk of supreme satisfaction, he watched Dallas's mouth fall open in astonishment. Next, he noted distractedly that her enormous eyes weren't focused on him, rather they were aimed over his left shoulder in the vicinity of the dressing room door.

Sensing danger, he wheeled around, uttering a muffled cry of surprise at the sight of the towering male figure with blazing steel eyes. Overcome with relief, Dallas and Teresa sagged against each other. They watched in mesmerized fascination as Rick crossed the threshold into the room. Henri charged the unexpected intruder. Looking rather fierce, Rick skillfully blocked Henri's attacking punch with his forearm, a split second later jabbing his clenched fist into the side of the Frenchman's jaw. Rick's other hand followed up with a powerful blow to the dazed man's solar plexus. With a loud grunt, Henri doubled over before his legs gave way and he sank to the hardwood floor.

Chapter Twelve

Breathing hard, Rick glared down at his opponent to make sure the man wouldn't be giving any more trouble. "Would someone care to tell me why this character was threatening you?" Rick's critical gaze swept over the wide-eyed females who were still too stunned to speak.

With a shrug, he leaned over, grasped Henri's shirt at his neck and hauled him to his feet. Dallas recovered her wits and began to explain in a breathless rush. Her pulse was doing double time from lingering fright, or joy at seeing Rick again, or both. She couldn't decide. As usual, he looked vital and handsome in an immaculate navy suit. His customary silk tie had been discarded, and his white shirt was open at the throat.

The police arrived within minutes. They roughly escorted Henri from the theater, but not before thanking Rick for apprehending one of Seville's elusive jewel thieves who no doubt would lead them to the rest of the gang.

"Don't thank me, *hombres*," Rick replied, wearily rubbing his jaw. "Señorita Jones here is the one who discovered Thevenot's interesting sideline." Dallas blushed when the officers gaped at her in disbelief. She shifted self-consciously beneath their prolonged scrutiny. Then she gave a little laugh when she realized they were actually staring at her costume. In the excitement, she hadn't had time to change and knew she made a curious picture in her frilly, colorful peasant dress.

After spending several more moments comforting a teary-eyed Teresa, who insisted she must go down to the police station to see about Henri, Dallas was finally left alone with Rick.

"I guess I'd better get changed," she murmured, suddenly shy. Her eyes glanced everywhere but at him. She turned away from him to locate her clothes, tensing visibly when she felt Rick's fingers on her shoulders. One of his hands slid down her arm before curling around her waist, and the other slipped beneath her tousled hair and fumbled with the top button of her costume.

"Wh—what are you doing?" she asked, her voice a croaking whisper, her heart in her throat.

"Helping you to change, *mi amor*." Dallas felt a melting sweetness invade her exhausted frame. Even in this dreamy state, she hadn't failed to notice that Rick, for the first time, had called her his "love."

This gave her the confidence to respond with a light approach to match his. "So . . . what took you so long?" she queried tremulously.

At that, she was twirled around and tenderly crushed against him. "I don't know why I put up with your impudent mouth," Rick muttered into her hair.

"That's it! Abuse a poor girl who's just been through a terrifying ordeal at the mercy of a deranged Frenchman." Dallas tilted her head back so she could meet Rick's laughing gaze. "I thought you were out of town," she added in a small voice.

"I was," he replied. "I'd just gotten to the hotel when Anita waylaid me in the lobby with the news that you hadn't shown up, and your aunt was getting concerned. I hightailed it over here and found that jerk getting ready to make mincemeat out of you." He flashed a boyish grin that took years off his curiously drawn face. Then Rick frowned, becoming abruptly serious. "I wanted to hurt him very badly for even thinking about laying a hand on you," he growled, his arms tightening possessively around her.

"Oh, I don't know," Dallas murmured. "I kind of wonder if maybe I owe him one." She buried her face against Rick's shoulder with a sigh of pure happiness.

"What's that supposed to mean?" he demanded.

She lifted her head and gazed up at him, a look of poignant vulnerability on the pale oval of her face. "I—I thought we'd never be together again, Rick," she whispered brokenly.

Surprise flickered in his eyes. "Never be together again?" he echoed, an inflection of amazement in his voice. "Keeping away from you has been my problem since the day we met. I was so afraid of rushing you, Dallas, but I couldn't seem to stay away . . . like right now." His mouth closed over hers, and the rich intensity of his kiss was a clue to how much he'd missed her, and how determined he was to make up for the days, hours and minutes they had been apart.

"Never be together again, hmm?" he said, his lips spreading in an indulgent smile. "I can't imagine where you got that crazy idea." His hands glided from her shoulders to her waist. Then he was caressing her back while pressing light kisses all over her face. "I think you bewitched me that very first day," he confessed, "when I saw you standing on the side of the road looking like a lost little girl. Right away, I was intrigued—not only by your beauty, but by your intelligence and your spirit—and that determination of yours to be so independent. That night, when you nearly collapsed in the coffee shop, and I picked you up to carry you to the room, I was struck by the strangest feeling—something I'd never experienced before with anyone. I didn't want to let go of you—I wanted to keep you in my arms. You seemed to belong there . . . close to my heart." By this time, Dallas was staring up at him, undisguised adoration misting her eyes. She felt weak-kneed and she had no words.

"I love you so much, Dallas, *mi vida*—my life," Rick said, gathering her urgently into his arms. "Did you honestly believe I would let you leave Seville without my having some say about our future?"

Dallas's cheek nestled against his chest. She was overcome by this impassioned declaration and deafened by the clamor of his heart at her ear. Through fluttering lashes, she glanced up to absorb his expression, awed to find it etched with tenderness. "How was I to know?" she asked softly. "You had gotten so cold, and then Anita told me you'd gone to Madrid again and wouldn't be back until the weekend . . . and that after I'd said I was leaving as soon as the last show was over."

"I had every intention of forcing the issue before tomorrow morning," he explained, "but I figured you needed some time and space to analyze your feelings. Everything had been happening so fast. I could tell you were a little frightened of me, but it was also very obvious how attracted you were," he gently teased.

Dallas felt a rosy stain coloring her face as she recalled her helpless response to his kisses—on more than one occasion. "That was one of my problems," she admitted timidly. "With my limited experience, I was so confused and afraid—not afraid of you exactly, but afraid of the way you made me feel. I kept telling myself it was just a—well, a physical attraction between us. To think Miguel was the one to wake me up to reality—and that awful storm out at the ranch . . ." Her voice trailed off. She shuddered as she recalled how terrified she'd been that day, watching Rick struggle with the panic-stricken horse. Rick insisted that she elaborate, so she did, telling him how Miguel had recognized the extent of her feelings even before she did.

"Remind me to apologize to Rivera for wanting to murder him," Rick muttered ruefully. "The minute you met the guy, I was sick with jealousy, imagining all sorts of things. I knew he wasn't above trying to seduce you—"

"Rick!" Dallas interrupted him, placing her fingertips over his mouth. "You've got Miguel all wrong. He truly was a perfect gentleman. He's been in love with Estela for years. He told me so the day we all went riding."

"Great ... I hope they'll be very happy." Rick pursed his lips to kiss Dallas's fingers.

"I—I thought maybe you were interested in her," Dallas admitted, lacing her arms around his neck.

Rick chuckled. "The truth is Estela and I are just old friends. Once in a while she enjoys playing up to me for Miguel's benefit. It's one of her little games. I figured it wouldn't hurt to humor her the day of the picnic—especially after our tiff by the pool." His smoldering gaze held Dallas's wide eyes.

"She did have some ... uh, some interesting things to say about you one day when we were with Miguel ... " Dallas's voice trailed off in uncertainty.

"What kind of things?" Rick asked, frowning.

"She thought she'd lost her diamond bracelet when she was lunching with you at the hotel a few weeks ago, and she said you were having the staff look for it."

"That's true."

"She sort of insinuated that if you couldn't locate the bracelet, you'd find some way to . . . to compensate her."

"Compensate her?"

"Yes . . . *generously*," Dallas punctuated after a moment's hesitation.

Grinning, Rick looked down into her flushed face. "You think I bought her a new diamond bracelet," he exclaimed.

Dallas squirmed beneath his teasing gaze. "Well, I noticed she was wearing a diamond tennis bracelet the day we went riding," Dallas declared defensively, "and you did wander off with her . . . arm in arm."

"Didn't I just admit to you that I was humoring her the day of the picnic? Primarily to get *your* attention." Amusement lurked in his eyes. "I guess I succeeded, hmm?"

"So you didn't buy her that bracelet?" Dallas persisted stubbornly.

"No, I did not buy her a bracelet of any description or any other kind of jewelry," he drawled. Then he turned serious. "You, my beautiful love, are the only woman I have any intention of giving jewelry to. . . ." He paused to brush a reverent kiss on her forehead. "In fact, I even have a particular item in mind."

A joyous light shone bright in Dallas's eyes when she realized he was referring to a ring. "Oh, Rick . . ." she sighed, tiptoeing to kiss him again. Her fingers threaded caressingly through his dark, disheveled hair.

"You really love me?" he demanded, making her

realize she had yet to say the words he was longing to hear.

"I love you and only you, *mi amor*," she professed softly, gasping when he flexed his arms around her in a grateful bearhug. Moments later he was gently unpeeling her from his chest so he could survey her glowing face.

"Will you marry me and live with me here . . . in Spain?" He looked extremely solemn. Dallas knew he was thinking about his mother, and how she'd never adjusted to life outside of her own country.

"I wouldn't dream of living anywhere else," Dallas assured him, "and, yes, of course, I'll marry you!"

"Mi ángel adorable," Rick whispered as his lips sought hers.

She eagerly accepted his grateful kiss, unbridled love for him radiating through her tired body and rejuvenating her. Warm blood raced in her veins, and sheer elation filled her heart with song.

Rick captured her arms and held her a little away from him. "I think I'd better get you back to the hotel," he said reluctantly. "Your aunt and my sister will be worried—"

"Oh, my gosh!" Dallas cried. "Eula and I have to fly to Rome tomorrow! I can't believe I forgot all about that." In dismay she searched Rick's face when it occurred to her that he may not want her to go— that he might not understand how important this trip was for her. Once again, as in many times since they'd met, she was caught in the grip of conflicting emotions. She didn't want to leave him now, but how could she pass up the opportunity to perform in Italy?

"What is it? What's wrong?" Rick demanded with concern. His ardent gaze held Dallas's anxious eyes, subjecting them to one of his direct, mind-reading probes. "You're not worried that I'll stand in the way of your music career?" he asked her, his tone mildly surprised. "I want you to be happy, and you have an extraordinary gift that should be nurtured and shared."

"Oh, thank you for saying that, Rick," Dallas breathed, wrapping her arms around him again. "It's just that I feel so torn all of a sudden," she admitted, close to tears. She rested her head against his shoulder. "I don't want to leave you. . . ."

"This isn't a competition, Dallas," Rick chided gently. He tugged on a silky strand of her hair so that she would look at him. "You don't have to make a choice between me and your career."

Her glistening eyes blinked at him. "I don't?" she said hopefully.

"Of course not." His teeth glimmered in a smile. "You're acting as if I'm one of those domineering, arrogant Spanish macho men," he complained in an indignant tone.

"You mean you're not?" She dimpled up at him.

"Maybe I am . . . a little," he allowed, a devilish gleam in his eyes. "Now, tell me about this audition and what it involves."

"Signor Bonelli said the auditions take place over a two-week period. Then, if you make the cut, they talk to you about specific roles, the schedule of rehearsals and the performance dates."

"You'll make the cut all right," Rick predicted with confidence.

"If I'm chosen for one of the principal parts, I could be in Italy for several months in the fall. . . ."

Rick saw that she was still riddled with indecision. "Would it make you feel any better if I went with you to Rome tomorrow?" he inquired gently.

"Oh, yes, Rick, please!"

"After your audition we could take the train up to Florence and pick out your engagement ring on the Ponte Vecchio," he said, referring to the famous old bridge housing tiny exclusive jewelry shops. "We could even visit the Uffizi Gallery while we're there."

"That would be wonderful!" Dallas declared, excitement bubbling in her voice. "So you know Florence well?"

Smiling, he nodded. "I spent an entire summer there when I was eighteen. The immersion in all that Renaissance art and architecture is probably what influenced my choice of careers more than anything. It's one of the most beautiful cities in Europe. I try to get back there every couple of years just to soak up the atmosphere."

"I've always wanted to go to Florence," Dallas said. "Aunt Eula and I had planned on spending the last week of our vacation there. Seeing it with you will be extra-special." Once again, her arms found their way around Rick's neck. He tenderly kissed her forehead, the tip of her nose, then paused an inch from her smiling, inviting lips. "If we start this again, I'm afraid we'll never get back to the hotel," he murmured. Snuggling against his shoulder, Dallas exhaled slowly. "You're right . . . we really should go." But neither one of them made a move to separate.

After a long silence, Rick spoke again: "We haven't talked about the wedding, *mi amor*. I expect you'll want to get married in Texas." Dallas raised her head to meet his questioning gaze. "But please don't make me wait *too* long," he implored earnestly. "I already feel like I've waited a lifetime for someone like you."

Dallas's eyes misted again. She felt like she was floating on a euphoric cloud. Could she ever be happier than she was at this exact moment in time? "I was thinking . . . a double wedding here in Seville would be really perfect," she said softly.

The expression on Rick's face made her heart dance. "I couldn't agree more," he said, "and you know, Anita will love the idea. Your parents and my mother and stepfather could fly over. Your aunt is here already, and I have a strong feeling she isn't going home anytime soon."

Dallas giggled. "We might have to make it a triple wedding, huh?"

"I don't care how many couples are involved," Rick informed her, "as long as you say 'I do.' "

"I do," she whispered.

Some time later, Dallas changed into jeans, sandals and a pink cotton top while Rick called the hotel. Anita demanded a blow-by-blow account of the hair-raising events of the evening. He gave her a capsulized version, promising more details later on. She, Tony, Eula and Roberto had been waiting up for them in the coffee shop. It was fast becoming an all-nighter for everyone.

Rick took Dallas's hand to lead her out to the Mercedes. He had parked it in front of the building. The wide tree-lined avenue was curiously quiet, due to the lateness of the hour. A sultry jasmine-scented breeze wafted their way from the nearby river. The midnight canopy of sky overhead twinkled brilliantly with starlight.

Rick halted by the passenger side door as another question occurred to him. "On the off-chance that you don't get selected for a role in Italy," he said, gazing down into Dallas's expectant face, "what would you like to do then?"

"You mean besides performing at the Met in New York and The Royal Opera House in London?" She smiled impishly at him, her heart skipping with incredible happiness.

He nodded, his expression a mixture of exasperation and amusement.

"Well, according to Miguel, I have a standing job offer here anytime I want." She gestured to the ornate front entrance of the theater.

"No pressure, *mi mujer*," Rick drawled with exaggerated patience, "but do you suppose you might manage to fit a baby or two into your hectic schedule at some point?" He grinningly reached for her.

"Oh, yes, definitely . . . at some point," Dallas murmured before welcoming the infinite joy and promise of his kiss.